PENGUIN BOOKS
# PANGEA

Talaiya Safdar has been a storyteller since she was a little girl, when she would curl up with her baby sister and swoop her off to lands with singing lollipops and rainbow skies. She spent most of her childhood reading, writing and daydreaming. She studied screenwriting and poetry and went on to study law. After practising law for almost seven years Talaiya returned to writing full time. She has consulted on dozens of screenplays and written over fifteen. She has also written, produced and directed several web series. *Pangea* is her first novel.

Talaiya lives in Scarsdale, New York, with her husband and her three children.

# PANGEA

## TALAIYA
## SAFDAR

PENGUIN BOOKS

PENGUIN BOOKS
Published by the Penguin Group
Penguin Books India Pvt. Ltd, 7th Floor, Infinity Tower C, DLF Cyber City,
Gurgaon 122 002, Haryana, India
Penguin Group (USA) Inc., 375 Hudson Street, New York, New York 10014, USA
Penguin Group (Canada), 90 Eglinton Avenue East, Suite 700, Toronto,
Ontario, M4P 2Y3, Canada
Penguin Books Ltd, 80 Strand, London WC2R 0RL, England
Penguin Ireland, 25 St Stephen's Green, Dublin 2, Ireland (a division of
Penguin Books Ltd)
Penguin Group (Australia), 707 Collins Street, Melbourne, Victoria 3008, Australia
Penguin Group (NZ), 67 Apollo Drive, Rosedale, Auckland 0632, New Zealand
Penguin Books (South Africa) (Pty) Ltd, Block D, Rosebank Office Park,
181 Jan Smuts Avenue, Parktown North, Johannesburg 2193, South Africa

Penguin Books Ltd, Registered Offices: 80 Strand, London WC2R 0RL, England

First published by Penguin Books India 2015

ISBN 9780143333494

Typeset in Dante by Manipal Digital Systems, Manipal
Printed at Thomson Press India Ltd, New Delhi

A PENGUIN RANDOM HOUSE COMPANY

*For my beautiful mother*

# Chapter 1

Insomnia. People who don't have it just don't understand what it feels like to lie staring at moon-painted shadows on the ceiling for so long that the abstract shapes start to look like people. An oily fingerprint on the window creates a winking eye. A fluttering string becomes a breaking smile. I could create a whole new world here in these sleepy, lonely hours.

And then there's the crying. It's not that it keeps me awake—it's more like I keep awake for it.

There's something about her cries. After being filtered through the walls of twisted metal and plastic that separate us, all that remains of every cry is just a naked, shivering, whimpering call to someone she knows and I know is never coming. The sound crawls into my chest and squeezes it until I can no longer see the winking eye or the breaking smile and I forget how to blink, how to hear and how to breathe. And that's when I can feel his arm at the dip of my waist slide across to my chest. He catches my breath and I nuzzle into him like a child curls into the shade of a rooted tree. I can't even hear her cries anymore. He does that for me every night even though I have no idea who he is, and I know that he is not really there. Maybe that's why I wait for her cries—because they bring him to me.

A glowing face projects on the plasma wall, illuminating my apartment in hues of blue. It shifts from man, woman, Asian, white, brown, black, short, tall, plump . . . it's a constantly changing face. It's the face of The People.

'Good evening, Ms Tygyr. We have received a request for authorization. A fellow Pangean citizen was found in possession of religious contraband—a text, prayer beads and a prayer mat. Religions and religious propaganda divide us and are violations of the Pangean law section 101.4. Those who do not enforce our principles weaken them. Please make your choice.'

There are two options: wash or release. Religion. Don't see that very often. I guess God is not that popular among the criminals anymore. I touch the virtual button that reads 'Wash'. I always touch wash. Everyone always touches wash.

'Thank you, Ms Suni Tygyr, for enforcing our principles. We are The People and we are one. United we stand. Divided we fall. We will integrate. We will repopulate. We will redistribute. We will survive as one world, one country, one race.' The connection ends. A dark silence engulfs my apartment. She's stopped crying. I close my eyes.

A sugary voice reminds me to charge my handheld, that I must be awake in seven hours and twelve minutes and that I have not had the recommended minimum amount of sleep in over three weeks and two days. I do not appreciate the reminder. I hold my eyes closed and replay scenes from the day over and over in my head, but this time I say the smartest and wittiest thing at the exact right time and my hair looks great.

Another morning. The sugary voice wishes me a pleasant Day of Creation. I open my heavy eyes to my cold, immaculate shoebox apartment. The brilliant sun mutes to a dull grey as it pours through my sunsafe-tinted Pangean windows. All my stuff is tucked away neatly in compartments, leaving all the shiny counters as barren as the desert outside. That's the Pangean way: everything has its place, a hidden place. I just want to open my eyes and see something that's mine so I can feel like I am home.

She's still at it, but it's fainter during the day—the crying. You wouldn't think noise would carry so much between apartments but it does. It's all these reflective surfaces. They bounce sounds around.

Toke will be here any minute. I find myself showered, dressed, lathered in sunsafe and brushing my hair before I realize it. After a while, routine takes over and you don't even notice that you're doing what you're supposed to. I look down at my crisp grey uniform—the same one I wear every day, the same one every Pangean wears.

Homogeneity ensures unity, while individualism brings destruction. But I still can't help wondering what it would feel like to wear red.

I weave my long, black hair into a thick braid. My braid—a heavy snake slithering about my back, tugging at my head and plucking at my scalp. Every day I wind it tighter, as if it's holding something together or hiding something inside.

Today will not be a run-of-the-mill day at work for us. It's the Day of Creation and all Pangean officers are called in for special assignments, so we only have time for one case. Toke will never tell me, and I will never ask, what they do on these special assignments but everyone knows it has something to do with the Uprising. That's just one of those things everyone knows but no one talks about.

It used to be different. Pangeans would get all dolled up in frilly grey dresses and shiny grey suits and trot around in the square celebrating the creation of Pangea for the whole day. People would dance in the streets while others would shower them with poppyfly petals from their apartment balconies. Boys and girls would disappear holding hands into the nooks and crannies of the shaded alleys between the tall glass buildings. Parents would parade their tots on their shoulders and wave the Pangean flag in the air. But now we just get some overexcited stragglers chanting and shouting right after the Creation statement. It's not safe anymore. Not since the Uprising. Risers are everywhere.

She has stopped crying. The silence is worse. I can see myself staring back at me in all these reflective surfaces. I'm not the typical seventeen-year-old Pangean. Today marks one hundred years since The Integration began and I don't look anything like I should. I'm darker than most and my large black eyes and thick black hair always make people stare. I don't like it when they stare at me. Toke says it's because I'm a different kind of beautiful. But I don't think that's what it is. I have seen others who look like me but mostly only in history books. Caged in labs and being poked and prodded with needles right after the sterilization began. The ones who looked like me were the ones in the cages and Seggies on the other side of the spectrum were the ones in the lab coats doing the prodding. They became sterile first and tested on my kind to find out why we could have babies when they couldn't. But then came The Cleanse and it didn't even matter anymore. Nothing did.

That's why they stare. I remind them of a piece of history they'd rather forget. A time with countries and races and religions that divided us and made us hate, fight and kill each other. Over one hundred years later and the world is all one country, Pangea, controlled completely by all Pangeans, The People. There are no religions and we have almost achieved one race. Almost one race if it wasn't for me and the other Seggies. The Segregated. There aren't that many Seggies anymore and when I see others I stare

5

at them too but not for the same reason that The People stare at me. I don't like all these reflective surfaces.

'Suni, I brought you a muffin.' Toke bounces in and kisses me on the cheek. Toke is fully integrated. He has warm, glowing light-brown skin and is of the perfect height and perfect build for a prestigious officer. He's been recognized by The People and has moved up the ranks quickly. Accompanying a lowly caseworker like me is way below his status but he doesn't trust anyone else to protect me. I should understand. He lost his last caseworker when a case turned out to be a Riser, a member of the Uprising. But of course we don't talk about that.

'Come on, slowpoke, you can eat it in the car.' He tries to look irritated but I know he's not. I follow him outside into the hallway of my apartment building. As always, he puts his hand on his stunray and puffs up his chest as soon as we're outside.

I pause at her door.

I have seen her many times: in the hallway, on the stairs, at the doorway. It's a small apartment building— only our two apartments on the second floor and two on the ground floor. I have seen everyone who lives here. We give each other awkward smiles, try not to make eye contact, and if we get cornered we talk about the weather, always and only about the weather. They are afraid of me.

But she is different. She held the door open for me one night when I was fleeing from the acid rain. She was still pregnant then. Even though my hands stung from the slow burn of the rain, I carried some bags for her up the stairs to the same landing I'm standing on right now. She broke off a piece of her live helder plant and told me it would soothe my reddening skin. It worked. She said her name was Fellie and we exchanged a few friendly words as she ran her hands along her protruding belly. Fellie was not afraid of me. At least she wasn't back then. But that was before.

Part of me wants to knock and offer something to soothe her but, unlike her, I have nothing to give.

'You should really report her.' He's right.

'She is allowed to mourn.'

'Excessive mourning is an indication of renunciation of the principles. It means that she's been unable to see the greater good—that it wasn't in fact a loss but a triumph.'

'She just needs time,' I lie.

'You said that last week.'

'I'll talk to her; she will understand,' I lie again. I cannot tell him that her torment has drawn me in. The dark fog of her anguish has enveloped me, making me feel lost, desperate, alone and hopeless. It's a horrible corrosive feeling but at least I feel something. It's the strongest feeling I have ever had and I'm not ready to let it go.

He nods. I pull myself away from her door and follow him down the twisted angular stairs, out of the pristine white building and to his car. There are so many exaggerated sharp edges in all Pangean architecture. They are weapons coming at me from every corner. But to others, they are works of art.

We hop in and he speeds off. I clutch on to the plastic door handle to try to stop myself from jostling around in the plastic seat of the plastic car. I guess we can thank the Old World for leaving us oceanfuls of plastic to repurpose. But gratitude isn't exactly what comes to mind when I think of the Old World. I read in a book that once upon a time people chopped down real rooted trees and burnt them for the smell. I don't want to think about those things yet; it's too early in the morning.

Toke drives way too fast on the dry, dusty desert roads that weave through the tall, shiny buildings. Their cold, straight lines and sharp-edged finishes are in contrast with the dry, barren ground. It's almost as if they were picked up from somewhere else and planted here. This is what the four cities in Pangea look like—deserts, savannahs and gorges sprinkled with clusters of shiny high-rises nestled between perfectly planned housing developments. Well, not real deserts. The sand is just a few feet deep and then there's rock. Miles and miles of rock. Here and there, amid the perfectly planned communities, they burst through the sand.

Every house, every building and every apartment are almost identical. Everything is new, clean and shiny. The People want it this way. The less there is to differentiate us the less there is to divide us. I suppose the problem is that the more perfect something gets, the less real it feels. Or maybe I'm just tired.

I forgot all about my muffin. It smells like sweet bananas and it's still warm. I try to eat gracefully but it's falling apart much faster than I can eat it.

'Did your mom make this?' I ask, annoyed.

'Why? Is it gross?'

'No, it's amazing but it's just falling apart. Not like your driving helps; I feel like I am in a blender!'

'I made it. Her fever was pretty high last night. She can barely walk around now.'

'What did the Expert say?' I mumble through a mouthful of muffin. He just shakes his head. He's not driving that fast anymore.

Toke's mom is thirty-six and she was pretty healthy before she got an infection a few weeks ago. He's lucky to have had her for as long as he did—most of us lose our parents before they hit thirty-five. Eventually they all get an infection. The oldest person alive is Chantee Chamomile and she's forty. I saw her last month at the founder's market, surrounded by hordes of people trying to get an autograph. I didn't even bother to try.

My mother died when I was ten. I remember holding my father's hand as the officers took her body away. I wanted to cry but I didn't. It was hard to hold it in. But I understood the Pangean way even when I was a child.

9

Then when my father died last year it was easier not to cry. The more deaths you live through the less you mourn. You can get used to anything.

'Have you tried the herbal leaves Ami gave you last week?' Ami is supposed to be a healer. She's been trained and has received the highest rank in her Academy. But I know for a fact that she has never healed anyone. If she's the best and she can't help anyone then imagine what the others are good for.

'Yes, I give them to her twice a day. They bring down the fever for a little while but it comes right back up after. She's going to end up just like Midnight, isn't she?' His voice cracks at the thought.

Midnight was a cat Ami and I found roaming in the savannah. Toke wanted me to take her to the Experts at the zoo. But they would have just put her in a cage for everyone to look at. I didn't want her locked up and it wasn't the law. She had green eyes and her fur was black and shiny, like my hair. I had never touched fur before; none of us had. She was like a little ball of magic, a unicorn, a fairy-tale creature from a far-off land. Something we shouldn't have, something we shouldn't touch and something we knew wouldn't stay.

Midnight was sick. An infection. The infection spread to her lungs. It exhausted her so much to try to breathe that she could barely do anything else. You could hear the crackling of the infection growing inside her when she let out her slow, long breaths. In a matter of a few days, her glittering green eyes had dulled completely. And that was the last time we held magic.

Midnight's death hit us all hard, but it hit Ami the hardest. She caressed the white spot on Midnight's forehead until she wheezed her last tortured breath. Ami recoiled. She drew her limbs in and rocked as the tears pouring from her eyes wilted her ruffles. Midnight had released something in Ami that she had been swallowing for years.

Ami disappeared for a few days after that. Toke thinks that she was unable to cope so she requested a partial wash to erase Midnight from her memory. He's probably right because the next time I saw her it was as if nothing had happened. We never spoke of Midnight again. Part of me wonders if she requested the partial wash or Toke reported her for excessive mourning. But there's no point in wondering because I will never know.

Toke turns his face away to blink out tears. I pretend I don't notice.

'Your mom is a tough cookie. She can fight this.'

His mind is some place else, some place dark. There's really nothing I can say to make Toke feel better. We both know his mother is dying and I've never really been good at this sort of thing.

'This is the best muffin I have ever had.' I over-emphasize my enthusiasm and it brings him back. He shimmers in a giant smile as his words sweeten.

'I'm so glad you liked it. Do you think I should make some to serve tomorrow?'

Tomorrow. Our wedding day. I don't answer him right away. He's the perfect guy for me. Our blood matches, he's respected and he makes me muffins. He's the good choice, he's the right choice and any girl would be thrilled to be getting married to him. But when I think of the wedding there's this ache in my abdomen, a dull ache of emptiness. Now my mind is wandering some place else, some place dark. I look out the window for something, anything.

There used to be so many more rooted trees here but they have died off slowly. It feels like almost every day another rooted tree's dried-up brittle roots snap into a poof of ash. It's the worst thing to watch. A magnificent creature thundering to its death, affecting only the sand in which its carcass sinks. Even the soil of the habitable regions is damaged from the nuclear fallout. Maybe that's why the tumbletrees just roll and never plant their roots. They know there is poison in the ground, slow burning poison that eats away over time. Over one hundred years later and The Cleanse is still killing. I can't imagine what the other continents are like. When I think of The Old World the word that comes to mind is: irresponsible. I have that pit in my stomach again. I feel like I forgot something or I'm missing something. Maybe it's the trees. I must just miss the trees.

'Sure. I think it would be great to have muffins tomorrow,' I concede.

We have arrived. The house is the third one to the left in a perfectly straight long line of identical townhouses. I never liked the townhouses. Something about living in straight lines and rows makes me feel like I am being harvested. But they are the newest additions to the architecture here in our Pangean city, East, and everybody who's anybody wants one. They are to be erected next in the cities of North, South and finally, West. West always gets everything last because it is the smallest city, with only ten thousand Pangeans. North is the largest, with almost twenty thousand people, and is home to the chipfin and other exotic wildlife. I have always wanted to visit North but Pangeans are not permitted to travel between cities. And The People have safeguarded each city from the others with impenetrable towering walls just to ensure no civilian intercity travel.

'We have about two minutes until the sandstorm so I'd rather wait it out in the car. I don't want to be in the case's house when it hits,' Toke declares. You don't want to have a case turn runner and have to chase them through a sandstorm.

You don't ever want to go into a sandstorm. You don't ever go into sandstorms.

Toke checks his watch and looks through all the windows. It's a long two minutes as we just sit in the cramped car and pretend we can't hear each other swallow until the first few grains of sand sprinkle the windshield. Within seconds the car is swathed in churning, whipping sand scratching at the glass. The screeches are so sharp and loud we can't even hear ourselves speak. Not that either of us tries. I suppose we can thank the Old World for this as well—violent, disabling storms that shred anyone in their path for exactly seventeen minutes and hit every day at the same time so they're easy enough to avoid. I guess that's what's so unnatural about them: their ineffectiveness and their punctuality.

And just like that, it's over and the Pangean sun blares through the sunsafe windows of the car.

As we walk to the door I pull up the case on my handheld and scroll through my notes. Joyli Pidgeon, eighteenth birthday today. Thirty-four visits in the last one year. Case has refused all approved candidates. Class: non-violent. No signs of being a Mark. The last phrase blinks: 'Request Wash?'

I know more about Joyli than most caseworkers even put in their notes. She, like us all, finished the academy at fifteen and based on her scores The People assigned her a career of farming but she had always dreamed of being a dancer. She never took to farming. She used to have nightmares that she'd forgotten to wear sunsafe and was trapped out in the farms, frying to a crisp in the sun. Stories have been whispered about such things happening to others but we don't speak about our carnivorous sun, how it gives life to the engineered seeds in the engineered soil of the engineered farms and how it never melts plastics and yet eats away at our flesh and has forced all wildlife to become nocturnal. We don't talk about these things—we just remember to wear sunsafe.

After a long day of seeding, she comes home and dances in her living room to a tune she plays in her head. She danced for me once. And she swayed like wheat yielding to the warm eastern wind, each long fluid movement pouring into the next with such continuity that even her hands, cracked, leathery and burnt from labour, seemed delicate.

I didn't even need to pull her case up but I did, hoping that maybe I was wrong and she had more time. I am not going to acknowledge that I want this to end any differently than I know it has to. This is for the greater good; it's for The People.

'It's a wash, isn't it?' Toke asks me, knowing I hate this part.

'Maybe she got married this week?'

'You don't need to worry. I'm here.'

Toke throws me a smile. My eyes linger on his face for a while. He's always trying to protect me. That would make most girls feel safe.

I stretch out each breath as Joyli opens the door. She's a tiny girl and looks more like a fourteen-year-old than the eighteen-year-old she is. She's frail and brittle and her beady eyes are further narrowed by her puffy-from-crying eyelids. I can tell from her face that she didn't get married but I ask anyway, hoping, again. She shakes her head slowly. I exhale deeply as I press on that blinking phrase and it changes to: WASH REQUESTED . . . PLEASE WAIT FOR AUTHORIZATION.

Neither Toke nor I will get this request for authorization because we are working on the case but every other Pangean will. Except, of course, for Joyli. Buzzes and alerts sound on handhelds and communication devices in the houses and street around us. Joyli hears the sounds and she knows what that means.

Everyone always presses wash.

She invites us in. Toke jerks his hand up sternly, signalling for me to wait. I comply. He always gets official at the case sites. He pulls his stunray, not gun, up to eye level, loads it and searches the apartment. Joyli poses no threat. He's authorized to shoot to stun only. Still, his gun is just a grasp away.

It's a long five minutes as he clunks around inside, opening doors and looking under furniture. He takes his time when he does a sweep. He always says that even the most innocent are hiding something. Joyli and I glance at each other periodically. Her glistening brown hair twirls in the light breeze the sandstorm left behind, floating up and settling back down in place. She tries to maintain eye contact but I just can't look at her for too long. She's lost and she is looking to me for something. But again, I have nothing to give.

I want to tell her that I am going to wash her today. That she will have no memory of any of her life and The People will create and implant new ones. The People will design a personality for her, decide whether she likes eggs or the colour blue, give her a washed blood-matched husband, they will love each other and live happily ever after. She, as she has always known herself to be, will die and be replaced with a content-upgraded version of herself. Maybe if I tell her all this she will take the wash voluntarily.

Instead, I slide my braid over my shoulder and let my fingers meander over the bulging weave and don't say anything. My handheld buzzes. I glance at it as the blinking phrase changes to: The People have chosen. The wash is authorized. Joyli sees it.

Her foot edges forward. She's going to try to run. I cannot allow that. It will make me look ineffective as her caseworker. After all, it is my job to predict this sort of thing and it will make Toke look weak as it's his job to prevent this sort of thing. There is no place for the weak and the ineffective with The People.

I put my arm up across the doorway and widen my stance. I look her dead in the eyes. 'Don't.' My voice is deep and stern.

She steps back and her eyes glisten with fresh tears. Toke walks out of the apartment and holds the stunray in her face. She trembles.

'Let's move inside.' Toke prods her in with the stunray.

We are standing in her living room, where she once felt safe enough to dance for me. Toke's search has left everything upside down, exposed and cluttered. Lying by my feet is the tiny clay ballerina I made for her last May. It's pretty hideous and looks more like a fat soldier than a ballerina. I am surprised she kept it all this time. I pick it up and struggle to stand it on its wavy legs but it keeps falling.

'It won't stand on its own. It needs to lean on something.' Joyli's voice is shaky. Her face is gripped with fear and her eyes jitter nervously. She brought this on herself and I must be comfortable with that. I leave the ballerina lying on its side and get a hold of myself.

'Joyli, The People have decided.' I'm trying to sound official, like Toke. Joyli's eyes dart around the room, as if she's searching for someone to come save her from me.

'Please, I just need some more time. I can't marry any of them. I will find someone. Please. Just another month. I promise I will marry by then.'

'You know I can't do that.'

'Yes, yes you can. They will never know. You can just tell them I ran or something. Please.' Her lips quiver.

'Are you asking us to disobey the law of The People? You sound like a member of The Uprising. Is that what you are? Are you a Riser?' Toke roars. I don't like to see him this way even though I know he is right.

'No! I'm just asking for some time,' Joyli begs.

This is why I hate this part. They never understand that this is going to happen no matter how many times I warn them. I have been coming to see her every week for the last year, showing her profiles of dozens of blood matches to marry and she rejected every single one.

I look at Toke and his face lightens a little, just a little. I feel that squeeze in my gut. It's coming again. It's the crying, I can't stand the crying. I have to be strong.

'Joyli Pidgeon, you have been found guilty of violating ordinance 104.5, which states that every person must marry a blood match by the age of eighteen. It is your duty to repopulate. It is your duty to participate in The Integration so we may all achieve one race. Your violation is an indication of your renunciation of the principles of The People. Your case was presented and The People have chosen. You are to be washed and redistributed.'

'No!' she screams. She grabs a jagged edged vase and raises it to bash Toke's head. Toke smacks the vase out of her hand and it clunks to the floor, landing by her feet. She jumps over the back of the sofa and heads for the door. I can see her using every piece of herself to be fast, to get out, to run. From me. Toke lunges over the table, knocking the clay ballerina to the ground. It takes Toke two wide steps and she's in his grasp. With one arm he throws her on the ground and holds her down. Her delicate limbs that swayed with fluidity as she danced wilt immediately under Toke's pressure.

He takes out the slim pen-like Washer and presses the dropper end into the tear duct of her eye. His eyes are cold and hard like stones and his lips, pressed together firmly. He looks disgusted by her. I try not to look at him.

'We are The People and we are one. United we stand. Divided we fall. We will integrate. We will repopulate. We will redistribute. We will survive as one world, one country, one race.' She lies helpless, twisted and frail like a drying tumbletree shrivelling in its resignation to the battering sun.

He looks at me. It's time. I nod and quickly look away. My eyes search for the ballerina but all that remains are dusty shards that sprinkle the floor. It's gone.

He presses the button on the Washer and with a click a gluey black drop oozes out of the Washer and into Joyli's eye. She squeals and blinks in a useless frenzy. It spreads, draping her eye with its glistening black shine and slithers under her skin across the bridge of her nose to her other eye. In less than a second both her eyes are covered and the black splinters into dozens of streams that snake under her eyelids, under the skin of her forehead and drill into her skull like hundreds of burrowing night ants. By the time all the black leaves her eyes, she's calm, quiet and her eyes are empty and blank. She's washed.

# Chapter 2

I slip into the car and watch Toke skip his way around to his side. I try not to look at Joyli sitting blankly in the back seat but I cannot escape her face. It appears in all the reflective surfaces. Only a few moments ago, her jittery eyes pleaded and searched for something, anything. Now her eyes only blink every several seconds, exactly and mechanically.

She's only at step one of the process. Toke's Washer only removed all her memories, characteristic traits and feelings. Higher ranked personnel at headquarters will work together with a Wash Worker and redesign her with new memories and a blood-matched spouse. She will be redistributed to a different Pangean city in a position they deem fit. Our job ends here and right now she is a blank, empty, hollow body, essentially lifeless but technically alive. I hate to see them this way. They look like walking corpses. But it's for The People. It's for the greater good. But tonight when I lie in bed and replay this scene over and over again in my head, I'm going to let her run.

'I bet they will make her a dancer,' Toke beams. His face is full of warmth and his eyes gleam. What a difference a few minutes makes.

'I hope so. I requested it in the report.' The People are generous with their washes. She will have all she wanted. Of course, she won't remember that she had wanted it.

'Do you think it will even matter if she's a dancer if she doesn't remember that it was always her dream?' I don't realize I said that out loud.

'What do you mean? Of course it matters! She's going to be a dancer! No more farming for her!'

'Yes.' Should I go on? No, I shouldn't but I do. 'But do you think it will feel the same? To hold a dream for years, to hope for it, to work for it, all that time and then you finally get there. It must feel like . . . flying.'

'Yeah?' He's puzzled.

'But if you're just given something without all that yearning, aching and working for it, it can't possibly feel as good. It will just feel ordinary.' I get lost in Joyli's emptiness and don't realize the gravity of what I just said for a few moments.

'What are you saying, Suni?' Now he's worried.

'What would you do if we weren't a blood match?' I have always wanted to ask him this.

'We *are* a blood match.'

'I know, but what if we weren't?'

22

'We have 89 per cent variation in our racial composition. We are from different races. We are a blood match.' He's getting official and he's right. We had ourselves tested months ago. There is no point thinking about all these hypotheticals. There is no point thinking so hard about anything. No good will come from that.

'Yes, you're right. I don't know why I'm thinking all this weird stuff.'

'It was a rough case; you spent a lot of time with her. It makes sense for you to feel this way. You'll miss her.' He's probably right. 'I think I am going to take her in to headquarters for redistribution myself. You don't need to be there. You should rest. I am going to take you home.'

I don't protest.

'But I did want us to be together for the Day of Creation statement. It will be our first one together.' He considers this as he says it.

'I think you're right. I should go home. It's the same statement every year anyway. That's the thing about history, it never changes.'

'Besides, we have so many more we can share together as husband and wife, right?' He's positively radiant. I feign a toothy grin.

For the rest of the ride home I stare out the windows, count the trees and think about how if Toke and I also had partial washes to remove Midnight, then it would be as if Midnight never existed.

I have not seen another car on the road today. Only Pangeans who require vehicles for their positions have them. The rest of us don't need them. You can walk to any point you would want to in East. Even so, it is unusual to not see at least one other car. All the other officers must be off the roads and already at their special assignments for the Day of Creation. Toke says that the Risers hit Pangea the hardest today because they hate our way of life and do not want to see us celebrate it.

Risers slither in shadows and hide in plain sight. They have positions in Pangea and look and act like every other Pangean. Most of us never know a Riser is one until it's too late. Toke is the only one I have ever heard of who has come face-to-face with a Riser and survived. He's not proud of it because he lost his caseworker. He never talks about what he saw that day.

It is said that the only way that some survived The Cleanse was through deceit, murder and pillaging done in the name of self-preservation. The Risers are the descendants of those survivors and they have the same brutality coursing through their veins. No one really knows what Risers do to their victims. There are never any bodies, evidence or witnesses. All we know is that if a Riser gets you then you vanish—as if you never existed.

Only four trees later, I am home.

'I'm going to walk you in.' Toke gets out of the car so quickly he beats me to it.

'Don't be silly. I'm right in front of the building—all I have to do is walk to the door.'

'Not today. It's not safe.'

'Okay, then why don't you watch me walk to the door?' With his eyes on my back I purposely shuffle my feet in tiny steps. It's absurd for him to think he needs to protect me all the time. But it's cute and maybe I do need it sometimes. I reach my building, request entrance at the plasma screen on the door, turn around and toss him a real smile. The door glides open as the plasma greets me in a sugary voice.

He can't resist; he dashes over to me and scoops me up in his arms as I drop my head on to his shoulder. He tries to kiss me and I bury my face away.

'We are getting married tomorrow and you still won't kiss me?' He playfully restrains and then releases me.

'Tomorrow is still tomorrow!' I tease and slip into the doorway. He pries the door open a crack, sticking his head in.

'I'm beginning to see your point about yearning and aching for something for a long time. All that was about this, wasn't it?' He is so chirpy and happy right now I don't want to take that away from him.

'Yeah, sure.' I mash his face out and close the door. I chuckle for a moment to myself and then stop when I realize that I just lied to him.

I climb the stairs in silence. Silence. She's not crying. I reach her door and pause. Is it true that maybe she only needed time to heal? Is that how it works? Time heals pain? I look down at my hands. I trace the faint pellet-like marks from the acid rain. Scars will always remain. From that look on her face when the officers took her baby, I can only imagine how deep her scar runs.

Her maddened eyes held on to bulging little pockets of tears, as if she did not want to let them see her cry. They snatched her baby from her clutching arms and every muscle in her face tightened and pulled as if they were ripping off her limb. Her teeth clenched, veins swelled, fists swung, legs kicked but she held on to those tears.

That was her second baby that was a Mark. So she knew when the officers came they were not there to redistribute the baby. Marks have no place with The People. Officers come and take Marks and we don't know what happens to them. That's another one of those things you just don't think or talk about.

It's rare that an infant shows that it's marked. It usually shows later on—when a child matures. But Fellie must have known it was a Mark when she was pregnant, which would be why she chose to have the baby at home alone. She even threw her husband out. She was able to spend a whole day with her newborn baby before I heard its little cries next door and reported her. Most mothers don't even get to see their baby's face. As soon as they are born The People redistribute the newborn to another and the mother will get another's child. *At least,* Fellie was able to spend a whole day with hers. You'd think that would have made it easier.

I didn't know her baby was a Mark when I reported her. I just thought she was trying to avoid her baby's redistribution. I was just doing what any Pangean would do. Redistribution ensures that everyone will love every child as their own.

In the Old World mothers kept their genetic babies. Experts say that it usually created a bond between parent and child, where the parent would place the child's needs above everyone else's, even their own. It wasn't until The Cleanse that the ugliness of that connection was revealed. The self-centred bond actually convinced the parent that the baby was more important than any other baby in the world. It warped all reason and logic. People were able to witness and participate in the slaughter of millions of other children just to preserve their own. Experts called this phenomenon 'othering'. The concept of identity difference created an 'us' and a 'them' and people were then justified in their minds to do whatever was necessary to 'them' in order to protect 'us'. Divisions and differences will lead to our destruction as it did to the Old World.

Redistribution unites Pangeans and if I had known that Fellie's baby was a Mark, I would have reported her anyway but at least I would have been prepared, mentally, for what I saw.

I had never seen a Mark's work before and from the expressions on the officers' faces it didn't look like they had ever seen it either. I got a glimpse of it as one of the officers scurried down the stairs of my apartment building with the baby in his arms. The baby was bundled in a fuzzy pink blanket embroidered with little sheep, all wearing pink bows. There are only three times in your life you're allowed to wear anything other than grey: on the day of your birth, on the day of your wedding and on the day of your death.

Fellie was a Seggie but on the other side of the spectrum from me. Her skin is so white it is almost clear and her eyes are the pale blue of a faded sky—so light it was almost as if she were blind. When I saw she was a Seggie I should have known she was a Mark. Marks are always Seggies. And even though all Seggies are not always Marks, it's better to be safe than sorry and steer clear of them.

Marks are different and differences are divisions that will eventually lead to our destruction. So Marks are the first step to our destruction. They are the product of the nuclear fallout—a mutated genetic side effect of the radiation exposure that left them 'marked'. That's why they only present in Seggies.

Seggies carry and express more of our ancestors' genes than the integrated Pangeans. That's why we look the way we do even after generations of participation in The Integration. The Seggies who also have their ancestors' mutation are Marks. We, the Seggies, are all basically expressed recessive genes. And if both parents share that recessive gene, even if it has not been expressed in generations it can be expressed like a dark family secret. The People have not found a way to identify one's recessive genes, otherwise that analysis would be part of the blood match. But the theory is that the more integrated the baby, the farther away it is from the mutation. That's another reason why The Integration is for the greater good. That's probably a large part of why they stare at me. They are probably scared I might be a Mark. Luckily for me, I am just as ordinary as they are.

I was standing on the landing between our apartments when the officer and the baby disappeared out of my sight down the stairs. But I heard it all. She started to shriek and her cries harmonized with Fellie's wails. Then a third voice screamed and threw off the melody.

I moved to the edge of the landing and peered around and down the stairs. I couldn't see everything but I saw enough. The officer had collapsed on the ground, shaking and screaming as he glared at his hands, scalded and bubbling with bursting blisters. The baby lay on the floor in the ashy singed remnants of her fuzzy pink sheep blanket with an eerie look of satisfaction. She looked past the carnage and at me with her faded sky eyes. Her face was still and she looked like she was thinking. Newborns aren't supposed to be able to do things like that.

'Burn them, Flora! Burn them all!' Fellie's trembling voice burst out from her apartment and slapped me with the realization that Fellie was also a Mark.

They were connected. That's how Fellie knew Flora was a Mark when she was pregnant. That's how Fellie knew what baby Flora did without being able to see it. That's why Fellie had birthed two Marks. Her Mark was her ability to connect with others. The officers, preoccupied with baby Flora, didn't recognize Fellie's Mark. But I did and for some reason that still eats away at my insides, I did not say a word about it.

Baby Flora understood her and started to shriek again. Her fuzzy blanket burst into flames, dissolving and exposing her blotchy newborn skin. One by one the officers tried to pick her up. One by one their hands would sizzle and their skin would melt away until there were no more officers who would dare try. Like a good girl she listened to her mother and she burned them all.

Then a man arrived and everything felt different. Even the air felt heavy. I tried to see his face but his back was turned towards me. He was not in Pangean grey but dressed in a deep black and there was something about him—something different, something powerful. He knelt down and gently caressed baby Flora's cheek with the back of his hand. He was able to calm her without burning. He picked her up and she nestled into his arms. She melted into a cooing, smiling baby in his hold faster than she melted her blanket. He walked right out of the building with her as Fellie's screams continued to pierce my ears and reverberate through my bones.

# Chapter 3

I speak into the plasma screen on my door to request entry. 'Welcome home, Ms Tygyr.' The door slides open and my handheld buzzes. I enter my apartment and hide my things neatly in their designated places as I listen to Ami's video message. She's dropped off my wedding dress. She's really excited about tomorrow and she warns me about the surprise party at my place tonight because she knows I hate surprises. I watch her brown hair bounce around her jumpy face as she bubbles and beams about all the details on my plasma wall.

'Listen, Suni, don't be your usual blah self about this. For The People's sake, listen to your only friend! Make yourself pretty and I'll see you in a bit. Kisses.' The video message ends. My eyes lock on to the beautiful beaded tulip-designed white wedding dress laid out for me on my bed. I feel my airways tightening. I pick it up and shove it into my closet, tightly closing the door. At least it's not grey.

I make myself a cup of tea and pluck some fresh mint leaves from my tiny plant and toss them in. I try not to think about Joyli and how she had swiped this plant from the engineered farms for me. Just focus on the tea. I close my eyes as I lower my face and inhale the warm, tingly steam from my cup. The smell is sweet and warm. This is what love must feel like. Warm mint tea.

Dull thuds from next door pluck me out of my moment. I consider investigating but my handheld buzzes and The People's constantly changing face projects on my plasma wall. I wrap my hands around my cup of tea as I sit on the edge of my bed to watch.

'Good afternoon, Pangeans of East, West, North and South. Today is our centennial Day of Creation. United we have survived, evolved and thrived. Today we remember all that has been lost and all that has been found. A day when we can celebrate our creation and our resilience and reaffirm the wisdom we have attained from the mistakes of our ancestors, their abusive dependence on medication and consumption of genetically modified foods that led to the worldwide sterilization. Their fanatic clinging to religious and racial divisions that led to the nuclear devastation of The Cleanse—almost destroying the entire planet and the human race. Almost. Out of their destruction came our creation. From the blood-stained ashes of our ancestors we, The People, rose and Pangea was born. And because of our principles we continue to thrive, one hundred years later!'

Shouts and cheers bounce around the reflective surfaces, resonate through the walls and shrink, slipping through the crevices like whispered secrets. The People are electrified.

'Pangeans. Please. Before we rejoice in our successes let us all take a moment of silence to reflect on this centennial Creation statement. On what we have learned and on what we must remember. Collectively as one.'

And the electricity fizzles away into a humming silence.

I close my eyes. I try to find the unity in the darkness behind my eyelids but all I find is solitude. I whip my braid over my shoulder and run my fingers along its bulges and valleys. Another thud. My eyes jolt open.

'We are The People and we are all one. United we stand. Divided we fall. We will integrate. We will repopulate. We will redistribute. We will survive as one world, one country, one race. Happy Day of Creation, fellow Pangeans.' The image then dissolves from my plasma wall.

I can hear people shouting and rejoicing outside. I get up and walk to my window. Some ecstatic Pangeans skip through the streets, and chant, 'One world, one country, one race.' Their elation is contagious and the crowd grows. This year pulled in a lot more than just a few stragglers.

Rejoicing over a victory breeds a deluded sense of invincibility. Or maybe they just forgot about the Risers.

I take a deep, long sip of my tea.

Another thud. I put my tea down and walk out of my apartment to Fellie's door. I put my hand on her door. It swells from within. I immediately drop my hand. I can hear clunking and rustling around. It sounds like there's a struggle going on. Somebody from the inside bangs on the door hard, almost shaking it off its hinges. The plasma screen on the door shorts, seeping out iridescent blue goo. The door slowly glides open.

My eyes take in one thing at a time. It's almost as if it's all in slow motion. First, I see Fellie's face. Her thin, black straight hair whips in and out of her agape mouth as she thrashes her head back and forth. She's on the floor and she screams as soon as she sees me. This is not the same scream. This one is mouthier. This is a scream of anger. Then, I see her arms pulled and stretched by three pairs of different male hands. Finally, I see them. There are three men and a woman. Their grey clothes have pockets bulging with objects and . . . weapons. Everyone freezes when they realize there's someone in the doorway. All four of them slowly turn their heads and rise as they lock eyes with me in an intense glare. The instant their eyes meet mine I know. They are Risers.

# Chapter 4

I know that as soon as I move my eyes from theirs they will lunge for me. I have no choice. I have to run. I turn my body and bolt for the steps. I hear them run after me. Their heavy feet stomp loudly into the ground. I bolt down the stairs, taking three at a time with long strides as Toke does. Toke. I slip my handheld out of my pocket as I reach for the door. I scream for help but the chants and shouts outside drown out my attempts.

I am almost out of the building. Someone will see me outside and help me. I hear their footsteps tumbling down the stairs. Their steps are getting louder—that means they're getting closer. They must be right behind me. I can't turn to look. I scream for the door to open and then I see the same blue goo dripping from the plasma on the door. I crash into the door and reach up to hit the manual door-open button. It swings open.

A sea of celebrating Pangeans rolls by the open door. They continue to chant and shout. Still intoxicated by their victory, they cannot see nor hear me scream.

I try to hurl myself out of the door but a hand snatches my braid at the base of my head and yanks me back inside. It stings and sends a sharp pain into my skull. I am being hauled back up the stairs. I watch the door creep shut as I am towed further and further away from the crowd. My body crashes into each step. I kick and scream. I hold on to my handheld tight and smash it into the hand dragging me. The hand releases my head and it slams to the floor. The hit was so hard, a loud hum lulls my head into fuzziness. Someone takes my handheld while another hauls me. I see the faces of the three men towering over me. The beefier one rubs his hand and narrows his eyes at me. I see their lips moving and their veins bursting through their temples. They are shouting but I cannot hear anything over my screams and the deafening hum in my ears. The girl must have me. I'm on the landing. My back scrapes along the cold floor. I'm in Fellie's apartment now. I see the Riser girl staring out the window. Her disinterest is more disturbing than the hands holding me down. Her red hair glows in the muted sun as she fiddles with the same helder plant that healed my burning hands. Who's pulling me then? I am released. I turn and see Fellie standing above me. It was Fellie. She jumps on me and punches me.

Her fist lands on the right side of my face between my nose and my lip. I can't feel the hit but I taste the warm salty blood filling my mouth. One of the men pulls her off and says something to her but I can't hear anything. All I hear is the hum. I can't even tell if I am screaming anymore. He pulls Fellie away and throws her into the beefy one's grasp.

He slowly bends down to my face. The hum fades as he looks into my eyes.

'It's her fault! She killed my baby! Kill her!' Fellie yells and struggles to free herself from the beefy Riser's grasp.

'This is your one warning. Back down. Understand?' the Riser by my face orders Fellie in a powerful but controlled tone. Fellie shrivels. This one has to be the leader.

The third wiry Riser has my handheld. He hurriedly pulls out a clear plastic bag of sand from a pocket. He frantically opens it and throws my handheld in. Sweat drips into his eyes as his twiggy fingers shake the bag vigorously. All the other Risers watch him, waiting. He opens the bag and pulls out my handheld. He tries to activate it. It's dead. He nods at the leader and he relaxes a bit as he brings his focus back to me.

The leader tries to touch my face and I yank away. He's a Seggie. His skin, hair and eyes are dark. He may look like me but I feel nothing but disgust for him—the same disgust Toke felt for Joyli.

'Let me go, you dirty Seggie!' I struggle to get up but he holds me down. I kick and try to hit him but I can't move. He's got me.

'It was not supposed to be this way. How could you let this happen?' he hisses to the other Risers through his teeth. They drop their heads and try to avoid his glare.

'You need to calm down. The more you resist, the harder this will be.' He speaks to me in the same soft voice I used when I spoke to Joyli before her wash. It's the softness that comes with the knowledge that you are in control of another's fate.

I muster up whatever I have in my dried-from-screaming mouth and spit in his face.

He smiles at me. Frustration flares like wildfire through my body and heats up my cheeks. I kick, punch, squirm, yank, pull and push. It's not working but I don't stop.

'I'm so sorry, Suni.' I stop when I hear him say my name. 'It wasn't supposed to be this way.'

He pulls something out of his pocket. It is similar to a Washer but instead of a dropper there's a lens. I struggle again but I still can't move. I think I'm screaming but I can't hear anything. He puts the Washer-like device on my forehead and a white flash of light blinds me. Everything blanches to white until there is nothing.

# Chapter 5

*With each step my feet sink into thick velvety leaves. I graze my hands on the tops of the brilliant purple, red, green and yellow poppyflies that teeter on their long, wiry stem legs and lift to flight as I brush them with my fingertips. It's a field of wild poppyflies. I am running. Not running from anything or running to anything—just running. The sun shines in and out of my eyes. I can feel my smile in my cheeks, my eyes, my fingertips. So much of this feels like a dream.*

*My hair, loose and free, flies around my face and trails like wings as I glide through the rising poppyflies. He grabs my hand. My body pulls into him. No, I pull my body into him. The sun glows from behind his shadowed figure and I nuzzle into his shade. There is no ache in my stomach. I am not looking for anything. I am not thinking of anything. It's as if the warmth of his chest has swallowed the world and me. This is what it feels like to feel safe.*

*This is not a dream.*

*I know this man.*

*I know this man.*

\* \* \*

My eyes jolt open. The warmth is replaced by an earthy chill. I'm in a cave. The leader sits beside me holding a cup. I should be scared of him but I'm not. His hair is as black as mine, as black as midnight. He coils up one of his curls in a finger and lets it spin out. His face is gentle, heavy and worn and his chin is bristled with a goatie. He looks tired. He extends the cup to me. Warm mint tea.

'I know you, don't I?' I ask.

'Do you remember me?' His voice is smooth and its warmth pours over me—but he's not that man. I shake my head.

'Where am I?'

He gently suggests that I drink my tea. I have no idea what is happening here but I don't think I am ready for it.

I look around. It's not a cave but it's underground. The edges and walls are blunt, as if they have been whittled down. Mounds of smooth rocks are scattered everywhere. Everything is brown and messy. There are no sharp edges here, no reflective surfaces, but it's cold, damp and dark. I can hear the chatter of others echo. There are so many voices.

'Una. A Riser Haven.' He extends his hand for mine. I take his hand without hesitation. Why didn't I hesitate?

He walks me through winding passageways into a gathering space. There are people with children. Families. Fruit stands, vegetable vendors, play areas, a school. People live here, in the cold, in the dark, in hiding.

'Are they all your prisoners?' He chuckles. I'm not sure why even I find the question absurd. These don't look like deceitful pillaging murderers who want to destroy our way of life.

A little girl in pigtails scampers over to him and attaches herself to his leg. Her giant green eyes fixate on me and shimmer in the yellow cave light.

'Is that her, Paltino?' she asks him. He looks at me and nods. Paltino. His name hums in my mind like the melody of a forgotten lullaby.

'All these people were washed by Pangea. We reversed their washes. We reclaimed them.'

'And me.' He nods. So it *was* a memory.

He explains to me that my memories will come back as my mind chooses and neither he nor anyone can force the process. For some, all their memories come crashing into them immediately and for others they reveal themselves in small pieces that you need to puzzle together to find yourself. It can take minutes, days, weeks, months, years. It all depends on when I am ready to remember as I control the reveal. It's my subconscious that chooses what I should remember and when. Some never remember everything because they are never ready to carry the weight of their truth. This is what my ache has been all along. I ached for the loss of my own self.

If they washed me then they constructed new memories for me. What part of what I knew was real and what part was constructed? When was I washed? Did I meet Toke at the university? Did Midnight even exist? Why do I count trees? Who is that man and why didn't the wash erase him? My parents. Did they really die? Air. There is no air here. All the questions, the empty spaces, the blackness, the holes swimming around frantically, scratching at my skull, gnawing at the back of my eyes—I can't breathe.

'Warm mint tea.' Paltino pushes the cup to my lips. I slowly inhale its tingly warmth. 'You know you like warm mint tea. So, let's just start there.' He smiles and just like that I can breathe again.

'So, *this* is it?' a raspy voice taunts from behind us. I turn to see the beefy Riser from Fellie's apartment eyeballing me with his dazzling blue eyes. He's thick and burly, with bouncing basketball biceps and a neck as wide as his jaw. He's clearly unimpressed by me. I dig my thumb into a tiny hole in the side of my pant leg. I wish I could crawl into that hole and hide. He scoffs and leaves.

Paltino apologizes to me—he does that a lot—and walks me over to a young man slumped in a chair and introduces him as Lute. His face is blank and his mouth hangs open. Paltino's eyes droop as he tells me Lute's story.

Lute was one of the first few reclaimed. He had so many questions, so much confusion. Paltino did not know better then, so he just answered his questions, reminding him of who he was before the wash instead of letting him remember on his own. But every answer led to another question until finally Paltino did not have any more answers and Lute was just left with questions. Paltino could see a hazy cloud engulf Lute and he has remained lost in that limbo fog, unable to decipher reality from dreams and past from present.

I watch Paltino shift Lute's position in the chair, fix his hair and wipe his drool. He repositions a crescent-shaped necklace so that it falls directly in the centre of Lute's protruding collarbone. How difficult it must be to have someone you care for become a shell of his or her real self and have no one else to blame but yourself. My mind wanders to Joyli's hollow eyes in the back seat of Toke's car. Warm mint tea. I'll start with that.

A meaty hand clamps on my shoulder and spins me around. It's a big teddy bear kinda guy with a jolly face.

'I'm Snap.' He has to bend down to shake my hand and his belly twitches when he chuckles. He elbows a wiry chap roping over. I remember him from the apartment. He's the skinny one who shook my phone in the sand bag.

'Doltier. We have been looking forward to meeting you—' Snap shuts him up with a swift nudge to the gut. They rumble a bit, spilling their drinks, chuckling and slapping each other in a typical man-love kind of way.

The Riser girl keeps her distance and checks me out from the corner of her eye. Her red hair is wound up into a bun and her sharp cheeks point to her thin lips like arrows. She circles the conversation but never joins it.

'And you're Paltino?' I confirm. The leader smiles, widely exposing a deep dimple under his right eye.

'It sounds nice to hear you say my name.' It felt nice to say it.

The Riser girl walks away. Paltino tells me her name is Malti. He asks me to give her some time but doesn't tell me why she needs it. Who was I? Hated by some and awaited by others? I sip my tea.

'Well, at least I wasn't boring.' That brings out his dimple again.

I watch the little girl who'd clung to Paltino scurry into a woman's arms. They are different versions of the same face, one bright-eyed and bushy tailed, the other tired and worn. It's her mother—her genetic mother! They don't redistribute in Una!

'Without redistribution how can you be sure everyone will love every child equally?'

'We can't.' Paltino coils up one of his brown curls on his finger and lets it spin out.

My mind wanders to Fellie's wails as they tore her baby from her like a limb.

I snake my way through the people—women running their hands on their pregnant bellies, stubby children's fingers painting on the rough cave walls, a brittle man crinkling his nose as he dips candles . . . This is freedom—dark, cold and messy.

I unravel my braid and allow my long, black hair to fall all over my shoulders, in my eyes, and trail behind me. I don't like braids.

# Chapter 6

*Yelp!*

*It's cold and damp. Another cave. Another yelp.*

*It's from a little girl in a red dress balancing on her mother's knee as her black hair is tugged, pulled and yanked into a tight braid. The little girl splays on to her mother's giant pregnant belly.*

*The mother's face is like my own . . . She's my mother, my genetic mother, and her name is . . . Serene. The mother and father I remember aren't real. They were never real. They were just constructed memories. I should have known that. I felt nothing for them. Even in the memories of their dead bodies being taken from me I felt nothing.*

*But now, I feel. I feel everything. A wave washes over me and I let that thought crash into me again and again. She's my mother. My mother. My mother. I want to drink her all in.*

*Her eyes are round and twinkly even in the darkness of the cave—the Old World's stars in a black sky. Her eyelashes flutter as she tries to blow a dangle of her hair from her face. A tiny droplet of sweat meanders down her slender neck and rests in the hollow of her collarbone. Her long, wispy fingers twine and twirl through the little girl's hair. My beautiful mother.*

'Oh, Suni darling, sit still, I'm almost done!' That's me. I am that little girl drooped over my mother's pregnant belly. Her lips . . . no, my lips pressed tight, eyebrows knitted, face hot with blood—this is what it feels like to wear red. She touches my cheek. Her buttery hands draw the heat from my cheeks and my face relaxes.

Her hand falls to my shoulder and her grip tightens as she lets out a yelp. I spin around to see her holding her belly as if it is about to fall and raking at the jagged walls for support. A slimy pinkish goo streams down her legs. She's having the baby.

The little me knows what to do. She must have told me . . . maybe we rehearsed it? I grab clean cloths, put water on the fire and shuffle my mother to a makeshift bed. She bites her lip to hold in her howls. She doesn't want me to worry. Little Me is not worried. Is this how she dies? Do I watch her die here in this cave leaving me alone with my face stretched back in this tight braid? What about the baby?

She squeezes her eyelids together and pushes with such force I can see veins bloat in her thin neck and sloped forehead. Sweat pastes her black hair on to her face and slithers down her neck and shoulders. I pick up her legs and push them back to her chest. I suppose this must help her.

'Mama, it's going to be okay. Just let him come in his own time. He knows what to do.' So much about what Little Me just said confuses me.

I move to her face—I dampen a cloth in water and wipe her matted hair from her forehead. She touches my braid, which has begun to unravel.

'My sweet beauty. I have ruined your hair.' She closes her eyes and drifts away. A baby cries. A boy. I slice at his cord with a blade and after a few slippery swipes he's free of Mama. I bundle him in all the clean cloths. Little Me is so composed even amidst all the blood, fluid and fleshy bits. Mama's still gone.

'Mama, he's here.' She does not respond. My beautiful mother.

'Mama, it is not time yet. You cannot rest yet. We need you, Mama.' Little Me rests the baby on Mama's chest. His eyes are wide open and his face is still. He blinks slowly as he cranes his head to look at Mama for the first time. He waits. I wait.

Her eyes flutter open and twinkle as she touches him. His face is round and rosy, like a bowl of peaches and cream. Not engineered peaches but how I imagine the real peaches from the Old World were, the ones that grew on rooted trees, each one a little different but also the same. His eyebrows scrunch up. He looks like he's concentrating.

'Hayk,' I declare.

'Hayk, a strong name for a little boy.'

'He won't always be little.'

49

*'People will hunt him. They are scared of what they don't understand. We have to protect him, Suni. We have to always protect Hayk.'*

*She pulls me closer and my now part-open hair tickles his cheek. He tries to grab it with his plump fist. Newborn babies aren't supposed to do things like that.*

*'He likes your hair down.'*

*'Good. I don't like braids.'*

# Chapter 7

The cloud of confusion and questions—where I am, who I am, how I got here—dissipates because now I have a purpose. This is what it feels like to belong.

'Where are Hayk and my mother?' I demand. Paltino just shakes his head. 'Where are they?' I yell through my teeth as I grab and smash a chair, leaving only a sharp, jagged plastic leg in my hand. I press the slivered tip as far as I can into Paltino's neck without drawing blood and shove him against the cave wall.

Other Risers try to lunge at me and I snarl at them. They back away, cowered. Malti stays cocked on the balls of her feet and never really fully backs down. Buzz's eyes ignite in blue. Did they just light up?

'Buzz, no.' Paltino orders the beefy Buzz and he backs off but not without displaying his protest with a kick to an empty garbage bin that plunks around for a bit.

'Where are they?' I couldn't care less about anyone or anything else in here.

51

'I cannot tell you. You know that, Suni. Just breathe, Suni. Just breathe.' He drops and slows his voice like one would do if they were talking a man off a ledge or to a child who unwittingly finds herself teetering on the top of a staircase. Even though I have the shard to his jugular he speaks to me as if he's trying to protect me.

I look at my fist, skin stretched tight and white, clutching the plastic dagger, and Paltino's shaking hands in the air. Where did that come from? I drop the stick.

My eyes scramble to find their faces—my mother and my brother. They have to be here. They have to be alive. The more I say it the more real it feels. We were in a cave; it has to be this one. It has to be.

'We have four Riser Havens. They are not in any of them.' Paltino tries to calm me by not saying much, as usual.

'Are they okay?'

'I can't answer that question.'

'Why can you answer some but not other questions?'

'I can only tell you what you didn't know before the wash or small details that don't really matter.'

'You're extremely annoying.' This brings out his dumb dimple again.

'It's okay. I'd rather you be pissed at me than the alternative.'

'What's the alternative? Me shoving this stick in your jugular?'

'No. Lute is the alternative.' Lute's empty shell gurgles in the outskirts of the cave. Maybe he's right. Doesn't make this less annoying. He chuckles. Wait, did I say that out loud? Why is he chuckling?

Okay, so the only way to find them is for me to remember. Right, okay I can do this. I look around for a seat and see the shattered chair. I cannot believe I did that.

I plop down on something, slam my eyelids shut and knock my fists against my temples. Remember. Remember. Come on, Suni. Remember.

'I think you need to hit harder.' A deep female voice. I open my eyes to see Malti. 'Maybe try a rock? Here, how about this one?' She holds out a large, round, sharp rock. A rock that would be perfect for smashing melons. Great, another exceedingly helpful Riser. Are they all just going to sit around and watch me? Don't they need to hunt chipfin or whatever lives out here with spears or something? A few chuckles. My face drops. I know I didn't say that aloud.

'You can hear my thoughts. You're all Marks!' I jump up and put up my fists, as if that could do anything against Marks.

'Not all of us are Marks,' Doltier defends.

'But most of us are. Yes,' Snap corrects. 'Tada!' His belly jiggles with delight. I'm not happy right now.

'Let's take a step back.' Paltino ushers me into a smaller cave, which is filled with towers of teetering books and a semi-clean bed. Dozens of candles line the walls—some melted, some lit. He rushes by a ledge and scurries to hide a few frayed photographs. A dangling light bulb zaps overhead.

'Why do you have candles if you have electricity?'

'I like fire. It's powerful.' Paltino's lips curl up in the corners like he's got an inside joke with himself.

'It's unpredictable, uncontrollable,' I scold.

'At least it's not boring.' I can't really argue with that logic. 'We weren't supposed to reclaim you yet. We weren't ready. I apologize for the messiness of this.' He's trying to protect me. He sounds like Toke. He clears his throat. Right, he just heard that.

'How long have you lived here?'

'The families live here, the children. But most of us don't. We all have roles in Pangea. We have to remain in the society to recognize other Marks and reclaim them. Some of us have high ranks with The People, so we have access to information. Information is power.' Toke was right. Hiding in plain sight. 'Another reason why I didn't want to reclaim you yet. Your union with Toke would have been beneficial. We don't have anyone that high up yet.'

'You would have let me marry him for information?'

'You wouldn't have known. Ignorance is bliss.' I did know. Buried deep behind Pangea's reflective surfaces in the tidy hidey spots was my dull ache and that man who never left. I did know.

'Why don't you just reclaim him?' I ask.

'He's been washed for too long. He'll reject it. There is a point when it's just been too long under the wash to reverse. But it's not an exact amount of time—for some it's years and for others it's months. We just don't know what makes some let go and others hang on.'

'How long have I been under?'

'A while. One of the longer ones.' Paltino brushes his chin bristles with his thumb.

'And you were going to wait even longer?'

'I knew you would hang on. You would never let go.' I guess I didn't let go.

'You're Marks. Just move boulders and part the sea. The People are no match for you.' There's his dimple again. It's growing on me.

'We aren't that powerful. Most of the Marks can just make pebbles hover, change their eye colour or make tumbletrees bloom. Can't win a revolution with flowers.' A deep cough at the entrance draws our attention. It's the beefy Riser, Buzz. 'Except for our modest Buzz here. The strongest Mark we have. Yet.'

Buzz leans up against the cave wall and uncrosses his arms along his bursting chest. 'Nice to meet you.' He extends his hand to shake mine. I guess something about me almost killing Paltino won him over. That makes me dribble a smile.

'Suni, watch that handshake. Buzz has a bit of a twisted sense of humour,' Paltino warns as I slip my hand into Buzz's, drawn in by his naughtiness.

'Sorry about your head. But it coulda been worse.' His eyes sizzle blue. He's the one from Fellie's apartment who dragged me up the steps. The one whose hand I smashed with my handheld.

'Right, well, sorry about your hand,' I bite back.

'Feisty!' Buzz appreciates the jostle.

'What's your Mark?' I test.

'Want me to show you?' He smiles at me and a sharp lightning bolt flashes in his eye. I jump back from the jittery jolt of voltage that he passes from his hand to mine.

'Buzz!' Paltino yells through his teeth and a badly hidden half smile. 'Sorry, Suni, I told you he has a sick sense of humour.'

'Electricity?' I rub my palm. It's a weird feeling, not pain in the physical sense but more like uneasiness—like extreme uneasiness.

'Psycho-electrocution, to be exact. I don't need to touch you to pass it to you.' Buzz pounds his chest and congratulates himself out of the cave.

'Modesty is not really his thing. But he's powerful. The most powerful we have seen in a while.' Paltino apologizes, again.

'Flora was powerful,' I remember.

Handhelds buzz in pockets. It's The People. It's a wash request and I don't have my handheld.

'I'm sorry about that. We had to deactivate it. Just in case someone noticed you were missing and tried to track it,' Doltier fingers his temple as he explains. 'We all have our handhelds—well, not all of us, just the ones who still have roles in Pangea. Anyway, we have our handhelds because no one tries to track us. We time our visits that way. But you were kinda . . . a surprise.'

'It's a wash request.' Paltino motions and Buzz, Snap, Malti and Doltier file in. 'Tula Beetle. Excessive opinions contrary to the principles. She's in West.'

'Let's go.' Buzz flexes his muscles.

'No way, man. You're hurt. You hang back this time.' Snap pats Buzz on his back. Buzz is about to react, overreact, when Paltino calms him. Buzz storms off but not without giving me the stink eye and flashing me his black-and-blue hand. I shrug.

Malti, Snap and Doltier hustle out of the cave. They are going to intercept the wash. That's what they do. They reclaim and they save. I smile inside, hoping that maybe they got Joyli too.

'My non-response to that wash request will be logged. It won't be long before Toke realizes I'm gone.'

'I know.'

Fellie drags herself in. Her swollen belly hangs, empty. Her eyes are dulled. She crawls into the bed, twisting her bony body into the greyed sheets.

'She's dead.' She weeps.

They kill the Marks that they take. Repopulation may be a founding Pangean principle but so is homogeneity. A Mark is a genetic trait and it cannot be bred out. The only way to eradicate Marks is to end their genetic lines. I think I always knew that even before I was reclaimed but I didn't want to see it. It's amazing how we only see what we want to even if we aren't washed. Maybe it is our minds protecting our souls from the ugliness. Ignorance is bliss.

I want to lie down next to her and swallow her pain in my chest. But I still have nothing to give. Apologies are self-serving and explanations are excuses. I need to carry this guilt like lead anchors stitched into my stomach. I should have known. *I should have known.*

'You could not have known.' She does not turn as she speaks to me. Her words slice through the air, sharp and strong. 'Not guilt. Guilt will cripple you. Pain. Own my pain. Own your pain. It will set you ablaze and your wildfire will spread throughout Pangea.'

Buzz surges in. 'Paltino, there's been a raid on Haven Four.' Paltino darts to leave when Buzz stops him. 'Everyone is gone.' Paltino's face sinks.

They stare at each other for a bit. I think they are communicating or maybe listening to someone else or something else. Whatever they hear drains the blood from their faces.

'They're here.' Buzz clenches his jaw and ignites his eyes as if he's about to pounce.

'No, Buzz. We have to evacuate. Evacuate everyone!' Paltino orders. Fellie curls further into the bed, knotting herself in the sheets.

Some people grab their children while others grab their guns. Buzz bolts away, scooping up as many Risers as his thick arms can carry.

'We can't leave Fellie.' I dart back into the cave and drape her skeletal figure around my shoulders. I hurry to catch Paltino. Her legs trail behind like feathery wisps.

A deafening explosion blasts through the back of the cave, filling the space with brown swirling smoke and dust. Fellie's limp body slips and disappears into the smoke.

'Fellie! Fellie!' A high-pitched ringing fills my ears. The heavy, hot cloud churns and twists into my lungs. Coughing, gagging, my stinging eyes flood with tears. I can't see. I can't hear. I can't breathe. My knees buckle and crash to the rocky cave floor. A sharp pain shoots up my right leg, followed by a crack.

# Chapter 8

*I examine my bloodied knees. It's a little bigger Little Me in a tattered red dress a few sizes too small that was beautiful once.*

*'Suni got a big boo-boo!' The chubby baby Hayk has stretched out into a skinny little boy. Pasty and bony. My bowl of peaches and cream has lost his peaches.*

*'You knew I was going to fall, Hayk, and you didn't warn me!' Little Me whines.*

*'Mama says sometimes you have to fall so you will learn how to be careful.'*

*'I don't care what Mama says!' Little Me's voice echoes through the tunnel and the words repeat fainter each time until they fade into whispers. Hayk tiptoes to a large rock—round like Mama's pregnant belly used to be. He circles the rock belly with his bony fingers and, with an apologetic nod of his head, points to where it leads.*

*'You want to swim?' Little Me peeks through the sliver of an opening and catches a glimpse of the cavernous space lit by the reflected twinkles of the sparkly blue pool at the bottom of the*

*fifty-foot drop. Little Me is not impressed. How many times can you swim in the same pool no matter how spectacular it is? After a while even the spectacular becomes ordinary. A cave is just a cave after all and Little Me wants to get out. 'We could pull the rock belly back and close us in and we could stay in there like secrets.'*

*I don't respond to Hayk; instead, I pull my bloody knees into my chest and hug them tight. 'Maybe we are too small to move this rock belly anyway.'*

*The air is stale and thick—it's suffocating. Both of us have paled and our bones are outlined in grey hollows. Little cave monsters. How long have we been locked in here?*

*Hayk pulls out a bunch of different leaves bound together with twine; solf leaves for sleeping, crickley root for fever and helder leaves for boo-boos. He puts the helder leaves on his tongue and his face twists up to his nose. Little Me does not let the bubbling giggle out. Dried helder leaves taste like dirty socks but they have to be wet to work. Not wet with water but wet with saliva. I tried water once when Hayk scraped his elbow. Anything to not have to put the dirty socks in my mouth. But Hayk didn't even think twice about it; he just slipped them in his mouth as if they were sweets. Hayk pulls the leaves out of his mouth, untwists his face and pats them on to Little Me's boo-boos.*

*'I'm sorry I yelled at you.' Little Me tugs the bony Hayk into her lap.*

*'I'm sorry I didn't tell you that you were going to fall.'*

'Mama is right. You can't tell everyone whenever something bad is going to happen. Sometimes the bad things are supposed to happen.'

'Everything happens for a reason.' Hayk stumbles on his words but is sure to get them out.

Little Me may be nodding along in agreement but I don't. Does everything happen for a reason? Do we ever get to find out what the reasons are? Because I'd really like to know what the reason was behind me getting washed. Me losing everyone . . . Me losing myself . . . I'm sorry, Hayk, I don't know if Mama was right.

Hayk peeks under the helder leaves and places them back. He pulls out a figure made of twisted twigs. It's a dancer. A ballet dancer. He folds it into Little Me's dress.

'What's this for?' Little Me brims over with the excitement of a surprise.

'It's time to run, Suni.' Hayk cups my face with his stick fingers, as an adult would do to a child. His black eyes shimmer and dim. I don't know why but I know I should be scared.

Mama bursts into the cave and grabs Hayk and me by our arms, her face twisted in fear. Her clothes are soaked in a mixture of sweat and blood. Hayk's face is calm and he smiles at me.

'Hayk, what's happening?' He ignores Little Me. 'What's happening?'

She pulls us through the cave like rag dolls, running, running through the dark. She trips and Hayk pulls my head an inch away from a sharp rock.

*Deep male voices shout from every direction. Little Me feels surrounded, suffocated, trapped in the dark. Lights from torches turn the corner. Mama tries to run but it's a dead end. Three Pangean officers stare us down. They look identical in their uniforms, height, build, bone structure. Like programmed robots marching to their written code. One grabs Mama and holds her to the wall. She screams and pleads with them to leave her children. It's that same deep wail that reverberates through my rib cage—it's Fellie's wails.*

*'Hold her steady,' the slightly bigger officer orders. He must be the leader.*

*'There are offspring. Two.' They aren't really talking to each other—just receiving and submitting transmissions.*

*Hayk places his hand on Mama and she calms, immediately. What did he tell her?*

*'He's a Mark. Get him out of here.' Transmit. Receive. Process. Mama and I watch an officer sling Hayk over his shoulder and leave. How can she just lie there and let them take him? We were supposed to protect him, always.*

*'Hayk!' Little Me cries. He does not struggle. He just waves goodbye and is carried out of the cave. 'HAYK!' A single tear breaks through Mama's eyes.*

*'She's just a Seggie.' The leader points to Little Me with his long nose. 'Wash her and send her in for redistribution.' Transmit. Receive. Process.*

*'No, please. She's young . . . she does not need to be washed. You can redistribute her. She will blend in nicely with any*

*family,' Mama pleads for me. The leader cocks his head and blows air through his flared nostrils. He slips off his various shaped and sized guns as he glares at Mama. The other officer releases Mama and steps aside. He's official, he's scary, he's just like Toke.*

*He walks over to Mama in two big, wide strides and slaps her across the face. Hard. She loses her balance from the force and falls to her knees. She grabs on to the jagged walls, scraping her palms, but quickly pulls herself back up. My beautiful mother.*

*'Kill this one.' Transmit. Am I going to watch them kill my mother again? Just as helpless as I was the first time?*

*'Please don't hurt my Mama. Please leave us be in this cave. Please leave us be!' I beg. This draws the attention of the leader and he begins to come at me until—*

*'Your wife is sick. I can heal her.' Mama talks over the leader to the other officer. The other officer's face drops. The leader sees the change in his posture.*

*'She's a Mark.' Receive. The leader brings the other officer back to his programming. The leader backhands Mama. His knuckle splits her lip and her face whips to the side. Blood spews from her open lip. Her wet eyes focus on the other officer as the blood on her lip slows, thickens and reverses to a syrupy crawl back up into the wound. Her opened lip slowly closes like a zipper. For extra emphasis she smiles.*

*'I can heal her.'*

*She can. I don't believe that she can. I know that she can. All of us, the leader, the other officer and I, share this moment of realization but unlike them I am not afraid. I am proud and maybe a little envious. But that's me—not Little Me. Little Me is scared she is about to lose her mother and suddenly so am I.*

*Process. The leader punches Mama in the jaw. Her chin snaps up and down and two of her teeth, pink with blood and spit, fly on to the officer's shirt.*

*'Let's see you smile now.' He arches his brow in victory until she does. The fact that he cannot break her seizes his body and he shakes in rage. Robots can feel.*

*'Just don't wash my daughter and I will save your wife,' she talks over him to the other officer—that's how small she has made him. The leader puts his gun to her forehead.*

*'Let's see you fix this, Mark.' His finger begins to press down on the trigger when his brains explode out of the side of his head all over the cave walls.*

*The other officer shot him.*

# Chapter 9

My bloody knees. No bones broken. What was that crack? My *spear*. I can still feel the singe from Buzz's voice. *Don't forget your spear.* I fling it into the grey cloud that has started to clear. But not enough. The smoke burns my throat and chest. Each wheezy inhale retches, twists and wrings my empty stomach. Or maybe it's because I have lost Fellie or because I lost Mama. My beautiful, powerful Mark mother.

Through the dissipating fog, shadowy figures emerge. Some running, some chasing . . . one grabs another by the hair . . . and rows of people are gagged and bound. Who are they? I feel another retch wind up in my muscles and I slap my hand over my mouth, sucking in little bits of air through the crevices between my fingers. Whoever they are I probably have moments before they see me.

A heavy hand flies through the smoke and tosses into my face, throwing me backwards. The hand tries to grab on to me, my face, my hair, my clothes. It's Buzz. The light from his eyes has all but gone.

'Help me,' he gurgles as something tugs him backwards into the fog. I don't know what to do. I twine my arms into his and plant my feet against a rock and pull as hard as I can. His dimmed eyes lock on to mine. He's scared.

'Hold on, Buzz. Hold on to me.' We try. We try but we can't do it. Whatever it is, it's too strong and the beefy Mark slips through my fingers like silk. Buzz. I lost Buzz. I lost Fellie.

What is in that cloud? *Suni, it's time to run.*

Chest to ground I begin to crawl, not knowing where I am going and who or what I am running from. I just crawl. Hayk. Where did they take him? They kill Marks. They always kill Marks. But if he were dead I would know. My body would know even if my mind didn't. I never lost him. He was always in me. In the dark parts of my head, the parts that grab me and shook me whenever I found myself following routines. Wake, dress, work, smile, eat, sleep. Repeat. He was why I couldn't enjoy banana muffins, why I always felt like I forgot something somewhere and why I gave Joyli that ballerina. He's still alive. He has to be.

A shiny object flashes, piercing through the cloud. It's blinking . . . no, twitching. Keep crawling. My shirt is now shredded and my belly drags and scrapes along the sharp, rocky cave floor. Keep crawling.

It's a necklace. A crescent necklace. It's Lute. He's on the ground; his body twitches, trembles then stills. I inch up to his face and reach his chest before I feel my hands wet and sticky with blood—his blood. He's dead.

I struggle to hold my scream in my throat but like rising vomit my body wants it out. Acidic, gurgling, salty scream. I can hear official-sounding voices and the heavy thump of boots nearby. Swallow it. Swallow it.

I slither off Lute's body—slick with blood—to the floor. Paltino? Paltino can you hear me? The boots are getting closer, the fog thinner, my breath shorter. Paltino.

I coil up between the cave wall and a boulder, tucking away my limbs like a snake. The fog is churning and clearing. Some things can be seen while others cannot. I can make out finer silhouettes. If I can see them they can see me. I tighten my coil.

Several boots clunk in unison. They are all in black, like the tall man that Flora nuzzled into, the same man who probably killed her. They can't be Pangean officers. They move together synchronized like a flock, their chins dropped. Their shoulders pivot and roll as they circle their prey. Hunters.

There is one woman, I think. I can't see her face but there is something distinctly feminine about her—her narrow back, her slender wrists. Something almost sexy. She drags the tip of her boot along the cave floor with each step. She bends down to their prey, swats it, plays with it and bursts into a pounce.

The prey is Fellie. The girl Hunter catches Fellie's neck in her claws and raises her skeletal trophy up. That's when I see the Hunter's face—it's Joyli.

Joyli's eyes, which were pleading and hollow just hours ago are now drunk with thirst. Her fluid labour-battered hands squeeze Fellie's neck. Her shoulder blades rub together in a comfortable sway as if she's winding up for something.

Joyli emits a mangled cry that swarms through the cave, crawls up my skin into my ears like thousands of night ants, biting, gnawing and scratching.

Fellie's neck reddens and her flesh begins to sizzle and bubble. Joyli's shrieks fill the cave and Fellie's face disappears in the growing sizzling skin bubbles. The smell of her cooking flesh singes my nose. Fellie. A few bubbles on her chest burst, sending layers of skin and pink blood splashing to the floor. Fellie. The smell.

Another Hunter walks over. He's the same one from Fellie's apartment—the tall man. I can't see his face but I know he's the same man. I recognize the heaviness in the air that his presence carries. He orders Joyli to stop. He must be their leader.

She immediately drops Fellie to the ground. Transmit. Receive. Process. But there's something more to them than programming and processes. There is something organic.

A hand grabs my arm and pulls.

# Chapter 10

*The hand yanks and jerks Little Me's body. My thin, long fingers coil around Mama's forearms—they don't even make it halfway around but I don't let go. No matter how hard that hand pulls at me . . . don't let go, Little Me, don't let go of Mama.*

*We are in a Pangean officer's car on a Pangean street. All the houses are identical, and are in neat rows with the same number and the same colour of poppyflies lining the walkway to each house. Little Me has never seen anything like it; the order and neatness of it all is a noose tightening around Little Me's neck.*

*Winged and scaled critters slosh up the side of a house only to slip and fall on top of each other, creating shiny, scaly writhing mounds on the ground. Chipfins. We must be in North. I've always wanted to see them. I watch a chipfin flubber its body up, splatter into the wall and slide down on its slimy, feathered scales back on top of his equally unsuccessful friends. They are just as ridiculous as I thought they'd be. A genetic mutation of a bird and a fish that neither flies nor swims. The books say* there is some irony there which I don't understand. They should have died out by now, unable to breed or feed but they are still here, defying all laws of natural selection. I suppose you can't have natural selection when everything is unnatural. Anyway, they just keep trying to climb walls, to get on top of houses. How many times do they have to slam their bodies into the wall to realize that they will never make it up there?

You see what you want.

Somebody's tugging at Little Me. It's the officer who shot his leader so Mama can save his wife. Kick and scream, Little Me, don't lose Mama, kick and scream.

She cups my face—forehead to forehead. 'Don't fight it. Everything happens for a reason.' And with that she tears my fingers from her skin like band-aids and the officer pulls Little Me out of the car and away from Mama. I've lost her.

Mama faces forward. She doesn't watch the officer carry Little Me away. But my eyes don't leave Mama, not for a moment, not even to see where I am being dragged. My cries fill the empty spaces of Pangea and bounce off the reflective surfaces until all the homes glow from inside and their windows fill with mindless blank faces pressed against the glass. Pangea, the land of zombies and robots.

We are in a house. The officer tosses me on to a sofa. A sofa. Little Me has never sat on a more luscious, squishy, fluffy mushball. She bounces right off on to the ground. Even under the circumstances this makes me laugh.

The home is Pangean clean. Grey, barren and shiny. Warm steaming food is carefully laid over the dining table.

*Little Me is very hungry. I ignore the plates and rip a leaf from a nearby plant. I fill it with rice and beans and scoop the food into my mouth in delicate fingertip-fulls. Little cave monster.*

*By the doorway the officer whispers to a plump couple with swollen faces. 'The new family whom she will blend with perfectly'—Mama's voice echoes in Little Me's head.*

*No, I won't be washed. No, they won't be washed but we will all love each other. The officer drones on. Came from a cave, on and on he goes. No siblings. No papers. I eat as the robots and zombies design the rest of my life in whispers.*

*I don't know these people. I don't remember them so they were washed from me. Why were they washed from me? Something happened in this house.*

*The door slams after the officer. My mother is gone. My brother is gone. The inflated woman sloshes over to me.*

*'Did you like the food?' I don't answer. Suddenly, she's next to me, her face too close to mine. Her perfectly round cheeks bounce like pink ping-pong balls as she twitches a nervous smile. The shiny-headed bald man puts his hands on hers and they tilt heads together and coo the way you'd imagine married couples do in storybooks and fairy tales. That's when Little Me realizes that even though this is their house and they are her captors they are just as lost and trapped as Little Me.*

*'Would you like some water?' The man's voice is sweet and soupy. He pours me a cup and Little Me downs it. So cold. Water is so much better cold.*

'Our home is empty. We tried for many years but we cannot have children. Pangea did not see fit to give us a child since we did not have one to give anyone. You are a blessing . . .'

'Lina!' The man jumps to cover her mouth, knocking some food down. Little Me scurries away and hides under the table. Religious terminology is forbidden. If Toke had heard that she would have been washed and redistributed. What did happen here?

'You are a gift. A gift.' She squeezes under the table with Little Me as she corrects herself.

Everything moves so quickly after that. They keep talking to me. Lina and Bearlett. This is the bathroom, the living room, the dining room. So much space . . . everything is mushy and squishy like them. Help yourself to anything. Would you like to take a bath? This is your home, so on and so forth. But it's not, is it? It's not my home, it's not my family. Right now, Little Me and I just want to go back to the dark, cold, suffocating cave.

Here's your room. Pinky, frilly. Don't let the bedbugs bite. Sweet dreams. Good night. Did they just have this room set up for a child that did not exist? How long did they have it sit here empty, haunted by the hopes and dreams of someone else—the coffin of their unborn child.

Little Me has never slept in a bed before. It's like a cloud. I just keep sinking and sinking, slowly swallowed by the pink, frilly blankets and dozens of accent pillows. You don't sleep in clouds and I don't like pink.

A chipfin flings itself through the window, smashing the glass. It flops around the room and manages to get itself tangled in the pink, lacy curtains. Its flat, beady golden eye darts around the room until it lands on me. It gasps for air through its gaping gills. It looks like it can't breathe but I think that's just the way it looks, like it's always just about to die.

Little Me walks over to the chipfin and strokes it. It looks slimy but it's soft. Its feathered buttery scales tickle the palm of my hand. I carefully weave its paper-wisp wings out of the lace, unwrapping it like a present until it lies naked in my hands.

I wander through the angular empty hallways that lead only to closed doors. Caves are much more efficient. One way in, one way out. What's the need for all these corners? Stairs. Mushy sofa. Door. No, there must be a back door. Back door.

After trying to push the door open for a few minutes without realizing the door knob needed to be turned, Little Me is finally in the backyard. The chipfin does not remove its flat eye from mine. I see the scaled mound of his friends slithering in the red moonlight. Before The Cleanse the books say the moonlight was blue. I wonder what it felt to stand in blue light—cool and sneaky. The chipfins' silver bodies would have shone and sparkled like gems in the blue moonlight, but in our red moonlight they look like the bloodied remains of a massacre. I suppose that is what they really are. Little Me considers putting it on the roof. But then what? There's nothing up there. At least right now they think there is. At least right now they have a purpose even if it is meaningless— they don't know better. I replace it back on the pile.

I watch the mound for a few moments. Watch them fling themselves into the wall and fall. Again. And again. Don't even know which one I returned—they all blend together in a bloody sea that rises and falls, repeat to infinity. They don't belong here. They don't belong anywhere. Now I see the irony.

A shovel. Little Me softens the grass under the tree and snuggles in under a pile a leaves. Little cave monster. Do I ever see Mama or Hayk again? I'm as lost as the chipfin. Worse. I'm alone.

Little Me pulls out the twig ballerina Hayk gave her and starts to cry. Hayk knew. He knew this was going to happen. Is that why he wanted us to close ourselves behind the rock belly like secrets? Was he trying to save us and I didn't let him? Why didn't I listen? Why did I let this happen? Everything happens for a reason . . . What possible purpose could this serve? Mama was wrong. There is no purpose for this.

A shiny object flashes, piercing through the black night. It's a necklace. It's a crescent necklace around the neck of a little boy, adorned with a pillow case as a cape and armed with a sword made of sticks. His pyjamas glow with rocket ships and falling stars and his face glows with deep dimples. The red moon twinkles in his shiny eyes as he bends down close to my face.

'You're not alone.'

It's Paltino.

# Chapter 11

It's Paltino's arm. He pulls me through winding tunnels worse than the hallways of Mr and Mrs Plumps' house until we are out in the dark-red night, running. Running. He stops at a pool of water in the middle of the desert. A cluster of tumbletrees somersault by. Another mutation—a tree that rolls through the desert, never planting its roots, perpetually in search for something, some sign of the world before. But like the chipfin they never find it. All that is left in this world is as unnatural as this still, moonlit blood pool in the middle of the desert.

'Hold your breath.' And with that short warning he plunges into the pool, me in tow. Underwater, he tugs me through a narrow opening that opens up into another tunnel. We pull ourselves out on to the rocky bank. Running. He drips water behind him. I slip and slide on the slick floor. I think I lost a shoe in the water. Keep up. Running.

The tunnel opens into the savannah . . . it's so cold. Pull aside a bush—another tunnel. That's how Risers move through cities and havens—through a network of disconnected tunnels so that if officers find one they find nothing. It must have taken years to dig these. How long have they . . . we been fighting? A jagged protruding rock slices my arm. Pay attention, Suni. Running. Open desert.

We climb down a gorge into a small carved-out cave that is the start of another tunnel. Battered plastic boxes and half-empty water bottles are scattered haphazardly. It's a hideout.

'This is where we wait for the others.' He gestures to a dirty mat and swaddles me, like a newborn, in a dusty blanket. He's trying to take care of me again. That brings out his dimple. A thick black spear of his hair makes a 'c' in front of his eye and pulses in the air of his quick breaths. He drops his gaze. I'm embarrassing him. That's cute.

He clears his throat and pretends not to hear me. He's been my friend for so long. How many times has he saved me? He chuckles as he fiddles around with a plastic box and spoons out a blob of goo.

He slops the goo in a shallow pit in the centre of the cave, coating it evenly and backs away.

'What are you doing?' A pitter-patter resonates through the cave as if it has just started to rain lightly. But it has not started to rain. Thousands of night ants rush to the pit and pile on each other, forming a giant ball. One by one they begin to glow until the throbbing ball is a bright red light like the moon.

'Officers would track a fire but not this. This is natural. Well, sort of. I guess the downside is that it doesn't give off heat.' In the new light he notices my sliced arm. He scrambles over, rips my sleeve and scrunches up his brow. I guess this is how he concentrates in tension. He's not even reacting to what I'm thinking. Hey, I think you can relax, it's just a cut, I might survive. Nothing. Bouncey bubblebutts bludgeon bumbling boobies. Nothing. Blah.

He scrambles to one of the little boxes and pulls out a few dried helder leaves. He softens them in his mouth and shrouds my cut. His face doesn't twist up like Hayk's. He must like the taste of dirty socks or maybe he's just used to it. I watch his spit mix with my blood and drip down my arm.

'That's gross,' I thank him.

'What exactly is a bubblebutt?'

In a cave, on the run, my arm covered in spit, lit by a giant throbbing ant ball—I have a friend. A real friend. But he's not that man. The man from the field, the man who was never fully washed away, the man who never fully left. I know Paltino is not that man. And as if I pushed him away, he retracts from me.

'What happened to Bearlett and Lina?'

Stones and pebbles shower the entrance to the cave. Someone is climbing down the gorge. Malti, Snap and Doltier.

'Buzz?' Paltino looks past the three. They shake their heads. Buzz is gone. But I knew that. I'm the one who let him go.

'We took the survivors to . . .' Malti stops Snap and throws me a look.

They all look at each other. In silence they have a conversation that they don't want me to hear. They argue, their arms waving, faces reddening. They look just as ridiculous as the chipfins. This catches their attention and they all throw a pissy look my way. Oops.

'You don't have to hide anything from me. What could I possibly do?'

'As soon as she showed up the havens get raided! You can't pretend that that's just a coincidence.' Malti does not even acknowledge that I am sitting right there.

'Maybe they tracked us through her handheld?' Snap's face has lost its jolly.

'No way. I deactivated it at Fellie's,' Doltier jitters.

'It couldn't have been her handheld anyway. They didn't just get Una. They got all four havens. She doesn't even know where the other three are,' Paltino corrects.

'All of Una? All four havens? What happened to the people?' I dig my thumb into that hole in my pant leg.

'Gone!' Malti hisses.

'No bodies?' Paltino's eyebrows knit. Malti shakes her dropped head.

'The kids? The babies?' No one says anything as my stomach swallows my sinking heart.

'Besides us there are twenty survivors. In total,' Doltier says. The weight of that slows everyone down. 'And they only survived because they weren't in the havens when they were hit. Like us.'

'What about . . .?' Paltino finishes the rest of the question in his mind and Doltier responds the same way. They are hiding something from me.

'What is it?'

'Bearlett and Lina were in Haven Two.' Paltino plods over and snatches me into a hug. I don't know if he's crying for them or for the many who died tonight. But he's releasing something that he's held for too long. Maybe he's crying because I'm not, because I can't, because I don't remember that I loved them. If remembering that I loved them will do this to me maybe it's better if I don't. Paltino rips himself off me and wipes his face with his shirt. Malti, Doltier and Snap don't even dare to look at him like this.

'Who did this?' Snap blurts, fully aware that no one really knows the answer.

'They are Hunters. We are their prey. I have seen the tall one before. He's the one who took baby Flora.' I burrow in my dirty blanket as if it will take me back to Mama.

'How could they have found us?' Paltino is asking me. Why is he asking me?

'They are Marks. I don't know if all of them are but one of them was for sure. The girl,' I reply.

'They are not Marks.' Paltino is certain.

'Well, I saw her melt Fellie's skin away with the touch of her hand. The same thing I saw baby Flora do to all the officers who tried to take her. Except for that tall Hunter. She didn't burn him.'

'They are not Marks. You must have been confused in the smoke,' Malti scolds.

'I saw her do it. And the thing is that the girl Hunter didn't have this power twelve hours ago.'

'How do you know?' Malti is still attacking me.

'Because twelve hours ago I washed her.' This slaps everyone in the face. 'If she had it she would have used it then. Joyli. Her name is Joyli. Or her name *was* Joyli.' What happened to her after Toke dropped me home? Well, look what happened to me.

'That's what we need to figure out.' Paltino peels the helder leaves from my cut that I had forgotten about. It looks better.

'The havens are gone. We all need to go back to Pangea to our roles. See what you can find out about Joyli.' Paltino dabs my cut with fresh water from a canteen.

'I can't go back. I am getting married to Toke in a few hours.' I swat his hand away. Malti storms out of the cave and perches on a ledge, just out of earshot.

'I know. Toke has to know what happened to Joyli after you washed her. He was the last one to see her. You have to try to get it out of him.' Paltino is way too comfortable with his delivery. He's only trying to convince me to marry someone for information. You figure he'd be a little weary but he's not. He's relaxed, like he knows what I'm going to do before I do.

'Toke would never reveal a confidential mission to me. He's all about integrity and principles. Doing the right thing. He doesn't break rules.' Did you know that, Paltino?

'Be resourceful, Suni.'

I look around at the ragtag crew: Malti sulking on the ledge, Snap rubbing his rumbling tummy, Doltier tapping his temples and Paltino thumbing the helder leaves soaked in my blood. Broken, scared and lost—they don't belong here, they don't belong there, they don't belong anywhere. Chipfins. I am the only lead to the Hunters. I have to go. I am going to go.

I guess Paltino knew that along.

'You will not be alone. Ever.'

No one speaks as we walk through the dark cave tunnels for what feels like hours. The red throbbing ant ball light shrinks in the distance until it looks like a lone red star in the black night and then it disappears.

The cave opens into a lit room. Everyone changes back into Pangean grey. Uniforms for their roles. Malti is a border guard, Snap a factory worker, Doltier a teacher and Paltino an Expert. I could have guessed that. There's even a crispy new uniform for me but unfortunately, there is no extra shoe. Everyone lops on sunsafe. The more the merrier. We wash, scrub and wipe away as much as we can of last night. Paltino flashes his dimple as he kisses me on the cheek.

'I missed you.'

'I did too, I think.' Am I blushing?

He throws me a wink as he opens a door to a cascade of sunlight—somewhere in that cave night had turned to day—and we all scatter into the grey Pangean streets. Grey. Clean. Angular. Plastic. Shiny reflective surfaces.

I walk for just a few moments, passing a flock of Pangeans as they select shiny red apples and glowing yellow bananas at a grocer's. The perfect Pangean fruit is engineered from manufactured seedlings and grown in fake soil in fake farms and plucked to be sold to fake people. I want to tell them they aren't really eating a banana. They are eating a scientific replication of a banana. But what's the point? They are scientific replications of people.

My building. All this time I was just a few steps away from the truth. I always knew this was not my life. I always knew there was something missing, that I didn't belong, that I didn't fit. Poor little chipfin.

I trudge up the steps and try not to think about my head smashing into them. I pause at Fellie's broken door and imbibe the scene: mangled plastic, shattered glass, smears of gluey blood. It looks like someone died here. I suppose someone did. Fellie. This time I have something to give.

I request entry to my apartment and the sugary voice grants me access. The carnivorous sun pounds through the sunsafe windows but even the strength of the sun cannot bring warmth to this prison cell. The wedding dress lies on my bed, noodley arms stretched out and the veil positioned where the head should be. Deflated faceless bride.

A Pangean weapon is on the floor. That's not mine—they don't arm caseworkers. That's why we always have officers with us. If there is a weapon that means there is an officer nearby. My non-response to the wash request must have been logged and noticed. The People must have sent in an officer to investigate. How much do they know?

I grab the gun.

# Chapter 12

*I grab the gun.*

*'Suni!' Paltino complains. It's a little teen Paltino hollering at a little teen me. His dimple is deeper, his brow is relaxed and his eyes are bright.*

*I've got a skip in my step, a wave in my hair and my cheeks are full of colour. In fact our eyes are so bright that you can clearly see the other's reflection in them. So much must have happened in the next few years to dim both of our lights.*

*We are in the Academy.*

*'Ms Gord, it's a triple thunder stac .63. It operates on a short recoil and delayed blowback system which yields faster cycle times. The chrome-lined barrels provide corrosive resistance to acid rain. Which is a useless feature. Speaking of useless, it does not require a full-hand grip to fire. It is also large and difficult to conceal.' I sit down, my large black waves bouncing around my back. Little Teen Me is smart but not exactly humble.*

*'Suni, you can't show off like that. You don't want them to notice you,' Paltino pleads.*

'Ms Tygyr, why are the corrosive resistance to acid rain and single-finger trigger useless features?' Ms Gord adjusts the sweater that she is not wearing but is resting on her shoulders like a cape. It sloshes whenever she makes her exaggerated turns.

Paltino warns me with his eyebrow.

'Well, Ms Gord, having a weapon resistant to acid rain is useless unless we have developed a way to make the user of the weapon resistant also. Not sure if it's going to matter so much to you if your gun still works while you're decomposing in the acid rain. As far as the single-finger trigger goes, I'm sure all the thousands of single-digit Pangeans will be thrilled that now they can fire a weapon too.' Little Teen Me is stubborn too. 'Tee-hees' sprout like mushrooms throughout the room but a new deep, hearty laugh from the rear catches Little Teen Me's attention. I scan the room. No new faces. I shrug it off . . . probably someone had too much sour pie and burnt out their vocal chords. Ugh, the cafeteria. Irritated sweaty cooks in hairnets slopping jiggly blobs on plastic plates on plastic trays with plastic cups and plastic forks. Welcome to the Academy.

'Okay, Ms Tygyr, clearly you are not a fan of the triple thunder. Tell us then if you are confronted with four Risers, what weapon would you prefer to have?' Risers? Even back then? Ms Gord slides her glasses down her nose and peers at me just above their rim. 'Well?'

I open my mouth to slap her with some wit but Paltino squeezes my arm. His eyes are telling me to stop. 'You have to be smart, Suni. Not draw attention, play dumb, slide by *unnoticed.' His whiny voice pokes around my head. Hide in plain sight. Fine. Fine. I'll stop only because he's so worried. Always so worried about me. I want to tell her that I wouldn't need a weapon. I am not scared of Risers. I want to tell her that I would take that triple thunder and blast out of here so I can find my mother and brother. I guess that's why he's so worried—he knows me, and I guess I have always been a Riser.*

*'Whatever you suggest, Ms Gord.' I take a seat in my prickly surrender.*

*'Liar.' There's that voice again—deep and slow, it fills the room like warm honey floating in the whispers and murmurs as everyone tries to see . . . him.*

*'Did someone say something?' Ms Gord is just as curious.*

*'Maybe if you came face-to-face with Risers, a gun would be the last thing you would need.' He rises like an old oak that I saw once in a book. Tall, wide, humbling.*

*His eyes are almond-shaped and lined with tight, black curled lashes much prettier than mine. They catch all the light in the room and bounce them back to me. I squint in his glare. He's looking at me.*

*'Oh. Our new student, Mr . . .?' Ms Gord's voice becomes abnormally high-pitched.*

*'Axalte Neem.' He's still looking at me.*

*'Okay, Mr Neem, please elaborate on your statement. Why would a gun be the last thing you'd need if you came across a Riser?'*

*In Pangea that statement would get you a wash and a redistribution but not in the Academy. The People encourage debate at the Academy. That way they can squash any dissenting opinions because the Pangean way is the right way and everyone agrees to that when they fully understand. The only reason one would disagree with The Principles is because one did not understand them properly. There is no other reason to disagree, ever. Once you are explained the Pangean way you will agree with the Pangean way. You learn that in the Academy. And you have to know that by the time you get out. Paltino says they encourage debate so that they identify who may turn into a Riser. That's why you hide in plain sight. Dumb it down. Blend. Never argue. Never stand out. Never let them know what you are really thinking. Mr Neem needs to slow down. He's still looking at me. His sharp-angled bones drop defined shadows on his face. There's something so heavy about his stare, about his presence.*

*'I would like to know what Ms Tygyr thinks.' Oh, he's cheeky. Paltino tries to keep me seated. It doesn't work. Paltino tugs my ear to his mouth.*

*'He could be a plant by The People. He's baiting you. Think about it.' Paltino. Always trying to protect me.*

*'You don't need a gun, Mr Neem? What are you planning on doing with the Risers? Have a tea party?' I throw it back on him.*

*'You didn't answer my question.' Is he baiting me or flirting with me?*

*'I didn't hear a question.'*

'Do you think you'd need a gun if you came face-to-face with Risers?'

'I always think I need a gun. In fact I could use one right about now.' This gets a smile not just from his mouth but also his eyes.

He walks across the room to me, keeping his smiley eyes on mine and sits beside me. I think my mouth is hanging open. I snap it shut. Am I staring at him? He runs his wide hand through his black hair and his thick spikes spring back to their original position. He leans into me so close I can feel the heat of his breath on my neck.

'Hi.' His deep voice vibrates through me, knocking my ribs together. He rolls back his big, round shoulders. Smiley Eyes is nervous. I feel a jittery heat scamper all over me. I lean and inhale him. Warm mint tea.

This is that man, the man from my dream, the man from the field, the man who calmed me every night, the man who was never truly washed from me. He is why I count the trees and why the light from my eyes is gone. He is why love is warm mint tea.

I knew this man. I loved this man. I lost this man.

# Chapter 13

Axalte. Axalte Neem. I swirl his name in my mouth and get lost in its taste on my tongue until I remember that there's someone in my apartment.

The heavy black gun rattles in my shaking hand. A sound from behind. I swing around. Nothing. Shadows flicker from beneath the bathroom door. Someone is in there. I widen my stance, brace myself and aim at the door as it slowly creaks opens. I close my eyes and fire the gun. Twice.

POP!

POP!

At some point in the middle of the second shot my eyes spring open. Ami ducks and screams. Ami? The bullets had landed about three feet to the left of her head. Not my finest moment.

'What are you doing, Suni?' Ami sprouts from the floor and stomps over, snatching the gun.

'I thought you were, I don't know. I just saw the gun and . . . I thought you were a Riser.' I am not sure what else to say.

'It's Toke's gun . . . don't you recognize it?' Her thin, poky hair wisps about as she whips her head back and forth . . . as if shaking it up will help her understand what's going on. She does that often.

'I'm sorry, Ami.'

'It's okay. Thank The People you're a really bad shot!' she cackles. Ami has always had this bizarre laugh that starts off like any other but then increases in volume and pitch range until it's a witchy cackle. It also doesn't help that she laughs at everything. I suppose that means she's generally happy. Or she's washed. 'Toke's been trying to reach you all night . . . where have you been?'

I stutter for a bit and maybe grunt a few words. Nothing meaningful.

'Don't worry about it. He wanted to send an officer over to check on you but I got him to agree to me coming over with his gun. Not sure what he thought I'd be able to do with that. So . . .' She wiggles her eyebrows and cackles away. Ami is fully integrated but is on the lighter side of the spectrum. Come to think of it, all 'fully integrated' are on the lighter side. That's one of those things I think I always knew but never thought about. I have a lot of thinking to do.

'So where were you?' She crosses her arms and taps her foot. I mumble something. I really have to become a better liar, quick. 'You were with that guy. The factory worker with the black eyes.'

'What? You think I would do that?' I titter at the simplicity of the thought.

'He *was* cute,' she sings.

'Unauthorized dating is a crime, Ami.' Hide in plain sight.

'Eyes like that are worth a wash.' Cackle. 'Okay, fine, don't tell me. We have bigger fish to fry—like the fact that you look like you just walked out of The Cleanse. Where is your shoe? Oh never mind. And giant dark circles under your eyes. We have one hour to turn you into a beautiful blushing bride.' She eyes me up and down. 'I better get some more supplies.' She scuttles out and in.

There's a lot of rushing after that. Rush into the shower. Rush out of the shower. Rush to blow-dry my hair, pull, curl, pin. My face is pulled tight as Ami tucks and binds my black hair as if it's going to escape her grip. It doesn't. It yields into a perfect, neat, slick bun.

Juice from a kierry to redden my lips. Ami reminds me not to lick my lips until it dries—kierry juice is poison. Plump red shiny kierry berries that burst with honey-sweet juice are poison. Not the kierry, just its juice. The smell draws you in like a drug and almost convinces your mind that nothing will happen from just one lick—just one taste. If you squeeze out its juice the kierry can be eaten safely. But no one eats the dried, chewy, sweet carcass. What we are attracted to, what we want is the wet poison. How Pangean.

'By the time Toke kisses you the poison will have evaporated and all that will remain is the colour.' She clucks at the idea. I can't even force a giggle.

Ami squirts sunsafe into my palm. 'Put it on your legs; this dress has a super-sexy slit!' she beams. I do as I'm told and get distracted by two scars on my leg—one like a teardrop and on the other side of my leg, a perfect round circle.

'Where did you get those scars?'

I remember falling down the stairs and pinning my leg between a nail and the jagged edge of the railing. But I don't think that's what really happened. The memory doesn't feel the same as my memories of Teen Me and Little Me. I can't feel the pain from the cut, I don't know where I was going when I fell and I don't remember the colour of the bandage I wore. That's where the washed memories pale to real memories—the details.

'Ami, do you remember Midnight?' I hold my breath.

'Who?' She doesn't stop buzzing about to answer. I grab her face. I need to see her eyes when she responds.

'Midnight. A black kitten we found in the desert. Do you remember her?' I look in Ami's amber eyes for some sign, a shimmer of recognition, a gleam of truth, a twinkle of regret.

'No, Suni. Let go of me!' She pulls away and shakes her head. There's nothing there. Nothing. She's been washed. I always knew that. I don't know why I bothered. 'What's wrong with you today?' There's so much wrong, Ami, so much.

'Suni, where were you last night?' Her eyebrows furrow.

Ami is my friend, my only friend. Well, the only friend I knew I had until yesterday. We are not washed to be friends; it just happened. Though I suppose I can't know that, but I'd like to think that's true. Something about her jumpiness always made me feel lighter. I want to tell her about Axalte, Paltino, the Risers, about my mother and Hayk. That there is something real out there outside of this manufactured plastic-land of ridiculous ironies and robots and zombies: a place where she can make choices and mistakes, a place where there are lovers and mothers, a place where she can remember Midnight. But I don't. I can't.

Her handheld buzzes. It's Toke. Yes, yes everything is fine. I'm fine. I'm thrilled. I lost my handheld in my excitement and just fell asleep. I look beautiful. We are on our way.

She's a much better liar than me. She marches around and stuffs me into the wedding dress, handcuffs me with jewels, ties me up with ribbons and jams me into the car, eyebrow V intact while she breathes loudly through her nose. And before I get to say anything to her we are there.

Pink ribbons float in the dry air like Fellie's winging limbs in Joyli's hold. Pink balloons nod in the bobblehead sea of the who's who of Pangean guests. I don't like pink.

Toke parts the sea and tows me to the official table. Four identical blocky men sit in a row, each with a contract, pen and whiskered grin. Holding the pen in the exact same angle with the exact same grip they push their pens forward to me at the exact same time. I burst out in a giggle. You can't be serious. Does no one see how weird this is? Bobbleheads, robots and zombies. Toke catches me in a confused glare. Pangean Suni doesn't giggle. My face falls. They are staring at me. They are going to find out and then the Risers will have no hope. I can't stand out, draw attention. I have to blend. Dumb it down. Find my inner bobblehead.

Block man number one. I smile, take his pen, sign and remind myself not to smile too widely for two, three . . . I pause for a second at four. This is what I have to give Fellie. I sign. Toke follows. His hair is shiny and sleek today. The corners of his mouth are turned up in a smile. There is so much he doesn't know.

And with four pens and a round of applause I'm married. Toke turns to me and parts his lips. He's going to kiss me. I push his chest back with my hand.

'The kierry isn't dry.' He places his hand on mine and raises my hand to his lips.

'It's okay if you're shy.' That irritates me. I'm not shy. He has no idea who I am. Cheeky, spunky, smart, flirty, sexy me. Dumb it down, Suni. Hide in plain sight. Think of Paltino.

'Yes, not in front of all these people.' I lower my gaze in chastity and roll my eyes in reality. There's my bobblehead.

Not releasing my hand, Toke throws me into the sea, steering me through the 'hellos' and 'thank yous' until he releases me to his mother.

Mrs Quail's emaciated frame slouches in a mushy chair. Her head hangs and her face is sunken with greys and yellows. The infection has ripped through her. I re-tuck a pillow here and there to try to support her wilting body. She waves it away.

'Don't fuss over me.' Her voice crackles and is as faint as a whisper. I draw myself closer to not miss one word. 'Look at you. Beautiful Suni. I don't think you know what you have given me today. I can leave this world knowing that my son will be truly cared for. None of this washed business. But truly loved. Peace. You have given my soul peace.'

Her words sit on my chest like a boulder, crushing my ribs, squeezing my lungs. I tip my chin down and try to blink the tears from my eyes before anyone sees.

One catches in my bottom eyelash. Mrs Quail raises her knobby hand and my tear disappears into the cracks of her skin. I'm sorry. I don't love him. I don't love him. I'm so sorry. She waves me closer and puts her dry sandpaper lips to my ear. She slips something cold and flat into the palm of my hand.

'Yes, you do,' she hums into my ear.

I snap up. She heard me. She's a Mark? All this time and Toke never knew? Her black eyes twinkle with the little spark of life she has left in her. Toke covers her with a blanket and scoops her up.

'Come, Mama, you should rest.' He carries her above the seething bobblehead sea to safety but her eyes never leave mine. I steal a glance at my hand as the sea approaches. It's a handheld. It's Toke's handheld. *Be resourceful, Suni.*

# Chapter 14

'Well, Ms Tygyr, are you going to say anything?' It's Teen Me. My hair, wet with sweat, snakes down my back and my chest races to catch up to my breath. I corner Ms Gord in a hallway. Be resourceful, Suni.

'I was wondering if you wouldn't mind explaining the significance of our last names again.' My eyes snap to the closed door of the lab and back to Ms Gord. I steer her away from the door—away from the flickering shadows in the lab.

'Oh, you know the answer to that. Pangean last names are all the living creatures that are now extinct because of The Cleanse. Now I must be on my way.' She shuffles to pass. Her cape has faded and thinned but still sloshes. I widen my stance so there's nowhere to go. For a moment she looks scared because for a moment I let myself show, but I catch and hide myself away before she can process it. This is not the time to show her. Not yet.

'I know that, yes. But I was working on the essay and I'm just really confused as to why we have to name ourselves after *things that are now extinct. I mean . . . like . . . why do you think we do that?' I turn my toes in, heels out, and tuck my hair behind my ear. Teen Me has this dumbing down thing to a science.*

*Ms Gord loves it when students are confused and bewildered; it makes her feel relevant. I guess I can't really blame her for that; in a way that's what we all want—relevance—and without it we become just another chipfin in the slithering mound.*

*She spews forth the theory that when we take these living things' names they exist in memory so in essence they never really die. They survive in spirit. Whatever that means. 'Surviving in spirit' is what living people say to themselves to make them feel better about death.*

*She loves to hear herself talk. Teen Me lets her run with it on and on—wait, I need to ask another question for clarification. Oh, what about this? Doesn't take much to keep the brainwashed vomit flowing—my eyes are on the shadows in the lab. Several questions and a few heaves later Ms Gord forgets all about the lab and shuffles back the other way.*

*I pull a black mask over my face and rush into the lab. Two masked young men shovel guns into backpacks. They turn and try to look at me through their unevenly cut out lopsided eyeholes. I can't help but giggle. Two different waves of warmth crash into me: Paltino and Axalte.*

*'Is that all?' I slide over, sling my backpack down and start cramming it. Guns, guns, Washers, guns.*

*'The heavy armoury is coded. We are not getting in.' Axalte's honey voice relaxes the muscles in my neck, letting my shoulders drop, even here, even like this.*

'We need to go. I think that hold you placed on the trip alarm failed.' Paltino concentrates on a plasma screen.

'What? That's not possible.' Teen Me flicks her fingers along the plasma, opening up folders with streaming numbers and codes that reflect in Teen Me's darting eyes. If I transfer the process the alarm will get trapped in a loop. Wait. This should work.

They tripped the loop? What if I interrupt the signifier with this trans virus? I understand code. I can break into any system, any handheld. Teen Me's face, illuminated in the plasma blue, falls. 'They know we are here.'

We grab our backpacks and look for the window just as the door swings open. Three officers, guns locked and loaded, start to shout.

'Drop the bags, Risers!'

We freeze. I am just a few feet from the closed window. Just a ten-foot drop. Just a quick dash into the desert and we will disappear into the sandstorm. We can make the jump and the run but not with that window closed. I need to break that glass. Paltino and Axalte drop their bags. The officers point their guns at me. I don't drop the bag.

I take one step to the side so I am directly between the officers' guns and the window. Paltino, let them fire one shot and then flip up that table. I know he doesn't like this plan but luckily this isn't the place or the time for an argument.

I designed this plan. I broke into the main frame. I distracted Ms Gord. It was my idea to steal these guns and use the sandstorm as an escape. That's why Paltino was looking at me for answers in the cave. Not because he thought I was responsible but because he was looking at me to lead. I am so much more than I ever knew.

'Put the bag down,' an officer roars.

'No.'

Transmit, receive, process. And without hesitation a gun is fired at me. I fall to the floor as the bullet buzzes across the room above my head and through the window. Paltino flips up the table and pushes his shoulder into one of the legs. Axalte joins against the other leg and they charge at the officers, ploughing down chairs, tables and officers.

I toss my bag out of the window and grab the other two before the third officer gets me. His fist lands on my stomach, sending me staggering back into the wall. Warm salty blood fills my mouth. I swirl it around and let it drip out. I pretend to be more winded than I am and fake a whiny cry.

I can't see Axalte or Paltino. They have jumped over the table on top of the other officers. I can hear shuffling, boots clanging and fists pounding skin. I just don't know who's getting it and who's giving it.

'Please, please don't hurt me. Please sir.' I slip my hand in the backpack behind me. The officer marches over to me and pulls off my mask. Now he's identified me. A thick vein pulses in his forehead. He feels like a big man now. He's going to be the talk of the town—'Brave Officer Snaps Riser's Neck'. His eyes are drunk with excitement. He clamps his hands around my neck and squeezes.

*I smile my mother's bloody smile and shove the tip of the gun I pulled out of my backpack up under his chin. Fear sobers him up, fast.*

*He releases my neck and throws his hands up. I've got him. Axalte and Paltino emerge, a little roughed up.*

*'Don't. He could have just been washed. It's not his fault.' Axalte slings a backpack on, pulls off his mask and places his hand on my shoulder. 'Don't.'*

*'He's right.' Paltino straps a backpack on.*

*'He's seen my face. I can't just let him go.' The officer cowers, now that he's face-to-face with a gun. How quickly a big man shrinks.*

*I slip the gun back in the backpack and pull out a Washer. The officer does not fight it. I suppose he knows that a wash is better than a gunshot. I shove the Washer into the corner of his eye and squeeze the black until his eye is covered. He claws at the black as it snakes under his face, forehead and skull, until his eyes widen and then fall blank and empty.*

*We stare at his emptiness for a moment, his still blank face, his motionless body, a living breathing corpse and realize that a wash is not better than a gunshot. I killed him. A wash is a death and not the 'surviving in spirit' kind. A wash is a true death: an unremembered, footprint-less, solitary death.*

*The thud of boots. More officers are coming. Axalte grabs the other bag and we fling ourselves and the bags out of the window into the thick, soupy desert sand. I scoop up the final bag, tread with each step sinking further into the heavy sand, suck in a deep breath and dive into the churning sandstorm.*

# Chapter 15

I understand code. I can do this.

I tighten my grip on Toke's handheld, hold my breath and dive into the bobblehead sea fighting the current—*such a lovely dress, so happy for you, congratulations, I remember my wedding day, smile for a picture*—and I'm at the bathroom door. It's locked. I flit around the corner into a small room and shut the door behind me.

It's an office. Grey, clean and empty. The lights buzz louder than they should. I sift through the handheld. Files. Archived. Search: Joyli Pidgeon. Status: Washed. Current location: CLASSIFIED. Current assignment: CLASSIFIED. He doesn't have the clearance. He's the highest ranking officer I know . . . if he doesn't have the clearance than who does? I have to get past this security. Can I bypass? No. Change the protocol? No. Realign the permissions? Yes, but it will be traceable.

A warm hand on my bare shoulder whips me around. It's Toke. He leaves the door open and a few bobbleheads wander in after him.

'What are you doing in here?' My cheeks heat up with blood and I can hear my heart pounding in my head. You can do this, Suni. You can do this.

'I just needed a minute. It's a bit overwhelming out there.' That's right. I'm weak and insecure Pangean Suni. Can't handle crowds or loud noises. He looks at his handheld in my hand.

'I couldn't find mine and I wanted to check the status of a case.' I swipe close the files and hand it back to him. I think I've got this lying thing down.

'Look at my bride's dedication to Pangea! Always working . . . even on her wedding day!' His belly laugh sends mimicked belly laugh ripples through the mini bobblehead sea behind him. 'I have a present for you. Close your eyes.' He sees my hesitation but insists. I don't want to close my eyes. Not here. I'm not safe.

They are looking at me. More bobbleheads pour in and join the gently swaying sea, eyes on me. Dumb it down. Hide in plain sight. I close my eyes. Black.

Something shuffles. Someone whispers. Some *ooohs* and *aaaahs*. It must be some sparkly ornament to hang around my neck as his claim of ownership, like a stake in the ground: 'PROPERTY OF TOKE QUAIL'.

'Surprise!' I open my eyes to see Joyli. Her face is still—not blank—but still like the surface of a lake that mirrors the sky while underneath it holds sharp-toothed creatures gnawing away at each other. I jerk my body away and into the desk behind me. 'Woah, woah. Suni, you okay? I guess you are surprised!' Toke bends down to my ear. 'Relax, Suni, she doesn't know you washed her. She's been redistributed. I had to pull in some major favours to get her here. I just thought you'd want to see that she was okay. That you did the right thing.' I don't know what to say or what to do, so I just nod. He helps me up. *Be resourceful, Suni*.

'Joyli, this is my wife, Suni. Suni, this is Joyli, she is a member of the Legion—the very prestigious, high-ranking new elite team of officers. She just married the Commander of the Legion yesterday. This is your surprise—that a Legionnaire came to your wedding.' Toke winks at me. Toke broke the rules. After she was washed and redistributed, no one from her previous life is supposed to ever see her again. She should have been transferred to another city. Toke, proud officer sporting his spit-shined badges, toothbrush-polished guns and shoulder blades tattooed with the Pangean principles—Toke, integrated Pangean dreamboat with the hair to match, broke the rules—for me. Surprise!

She congratulates me on my wedding. I congratulate her on hers. Neither of us seems particularly genuine but no one notices.

'Where is the Commander?' Toke interrupts our thrilling exchange. The Commander must have been the tall man. The one who carried the heaviness in the air. The one who did not burn when he took baby Flora, the one who stopped Joyli from killing Fellie. The thought makes me shudder.

'He is on an assignment,' Joyli responds in a monotone voice. Transmit, receive, process.

'I have not heard of The Legion . . .?' I am not sure if I should just ask a question outright but I want to bring it up somehow so I kind of turn a statement into a question by raising my voice at the end. Ridiculous.

'We are new.' Joyli flattens her black uniform covered in sleek pockets and well-positioned zippers. It's black. It's different. Pangea doesn't do different. Something is very wrong here. 'Created in response to the new Riser surges.'

What new Riser surges? She's lying.

'Although with all the progress The Legion has had in just the few days that it's been created I don't think there will be any Risers left. The Hunters!' Toke rocks on his heels in pride. Bobbleheads concur.

'The Commander and I really like that nickname. Hunters.' Joyli swoons at some memory swimming around in her head. Some fake planted memory. What have they done to her? Reduced to another ridiculous irony that belongs nowhere: a tree with no roots, a half-fish half-bird that can neither swim nor fly, a delectable poisonous berry lipstick and a murderous ballerina.

'It was nice to meet you, Mrs Quail.' That's right, I'm not Ms Tygyr. I just got married. I'm not sure which is harder to digest. 'But I really must be going.'

She can't leave yet—I need more information. I need something, anything. I have to do something. She must have a handheld.

Toke and Joyli argue for a few moments on staying for cake, just long enough for me to see the corner of her handheld jutting out from a zipper on her right side. Everything would be in that handheld. Be resourceful, Suni. Toke wins the argument and I throw my arms around Joyli—*slip her handheld out of her pocket*—in an unwarranted hug, not knowing if the hug will melt my skin. It does not.

Everyone's eyes are on me. Pangean Suni does not hug. But the weak and insecure Pangean Suni is overjoyed with the surprise that her new husband gave her. All this activity has her flushed and she needs to lie down now. They buy it. Bobbleheads nod and follow Toke and Joyli to the cake, leaving me alone in the office with Joyli's phone.

I swipe, search, sort. Locked. Classified. I can't get into her handheld without breaking its code and then it will be traceable—traceable back to Toke. He lied and arranged

for her presence here. They will assume he was involved.
He broke the rules for me. I can't do that to him. But . . .
But this is all we have left. Without this we have nothing,
no lead to the Hunters, no lead to all the Risers that were
taken—the babies, the kids. I can't let them take the Risers,
not like Flora. I can't just let them do this. I won't let them
do this.

# Chapter 16

*'I won't let them do this.' Teen Me grabs on to Paltino. 'You hear me? I won't!' Sand in our hair, clothes, ears, fingernails and eyelashes.*

*Axalte and Paltino rip through the shredded bags. Nothing.*

*'You can't. We can't stop them without the guns.' Paltino tears at his hair. The sandstorm snatched away all the guns and the hope that they brought with them. Sand flutters from my eyelashes into my eyes and gnaws, chews and burns until I buckle over.*

*Axalte cups my face in his hands as delicately as one would hold a wish and blows his sweet, cool breath into my blistering eyes and they flood with tears, flushing out the sand. The tears don't stop long after the sand is gone. Something about the pain that they unleash soothes my soul more than they soothe my eyes, and they pour, and pour. Pour for my mother, for my brother, for the poisoned grounds, for the rootless trees, for the forgotten washed, for the ridiculous chipfin, for the spiritless officer, for the lost guns, for Lute.*

*Lute. This is all for Lute, the blank boy in the wheelchair in Una with the crescent necklace. The first one reclaimed by the Risers. He was Paltino's brother. He is Paltino's brother. I remember.*

*Theory class. Ms Gord is scribbling some nonsense on the board. Lute won't let it go. Something about luck. Belief in the existence of luck is against Pangean principles. 'You are in control of your actions; you are in control of everything that you do and everything that happens to you. Everything that you do that fails is because of your shortcomings and everything that you do that succeeds is because of your greatness.'*

*They want us to believe that so that we run harder on their exercise wheels, so that we work in the fields until our hands crack, so that we follow the routine—wake, eat, work, procreate, sleep, repeat, infinity. So that we don't think, so that we don't question, so that we don't see that the control is just an illusion and we are just wooden puppets that believe that we are real. They have the control, they have always had the control.*

*Lute couldn't let it go. He pushed and pushed.*

*'We are here for a purpose. A greater purpose. And we will not be measured by our individual successes and failures but by our contributions to the advancement of humanity. We are all pieces of a puzzle; individually our struggles mean nothing but together our pain creates a beautiful picture. A picture, Ms Gord, that you will never see because, unlike me, you have no faith.'*

*He slowly sits down, cheeks fat with relief. I could almost feel the draft from his deep exhale. So many years of suffocating behind the mask, swallowing his words, blinking away his tears, controlling, planning, hiding, lying . . . he tore each layer off. And for that short moment we all shared his nakedness. For that short moment.*

*I remember.*

*They are coming to Paltino's home to wash and redistribute him. This was all for Lute . . . to save him. My tears pour for Lute.*

*'We don't have time to waste on this. They will be there any minute. We have to go now and get him out.' I shake the sand from my hair.*

*'He won't leave, Suni. He thinks this is his purpose.' Paltino does not bother to get rid of the sand—he just sits in it, allows it to furrow into his pores and rankle. He touches his neck to make sure his crescent necklace is still there. 'You think there are still stars up there?' Paltino looks up at the pinkening sky like a hurt child looks up at his mother hoping she can make the pain go away.*

*'I don't know, Paltino. I hope so.'*

*'He always told me that they were there. We just couldn't see them anymore because of the smog. But one day we were going to clean the sky and then we would see them again. The stars. He always told me that as long as those stars are up there we can undo what we have done. You know why I think we can't see the stars? Because they are gone. They are dead. We killed them like we killed God and like we killed everything else. There is no going back, there is no hope, there is no faith, there is no*

luck, all there is is an empty black sky and a moon painted red with our blood.'

We try not to think about what Paltino said as we slink into a cave that leads to a tunnel. We can't think like that. We need hope. There is nothing without hope. Running in the black winding tunnels is easy, comfortable; I fly through them anticipating each jutting rock, each uneven floor, each low-hanging boulder. The maps of these tunnels are etched into my mind and we blindly swoop through them in the dark. So different from when Paltino and I escaped the Hunters. I didn't know me then. Well, I didn't know this me then. The real me, the smart, clever, spunky, sexy, computer-hacking, officer-washing, plan-making, tunnel-running me. The only me that I knew just watched Lute die in the cave, but the real me risked everything I had to save him.

We are out. Paltino's house is ahead. Third one over in the long line of identical houses with identical roofs adorned with identical poppyflies. Stop.

We are too late. Six officers surround Lute outside his home. They never send six officers; they must have expected something. They tilt Lute's head up and bring the Washer to his eye. The black glops into his eyes and he does not struggle. He just sits there maskless, naked and fat with the satisfaction that he has served his purpose. If only we had the faith he had.

Paltino tries to go to Lute but Axalte and I hang on to him.

'Let me go!' he shouts through his teeth. He squirms and jerks his body, as sand flies through the air. Paltino, you have always been the rational one. Think before you act, keep calm and remember the bigger picture. Now I need you to hear that. You can't do anything for him. But he doesn't hear me when he doesn't want to. The corrosive ache of loss has already eaten through him. We cannot hold him down and he slips away like a whispered secret.

He takes three officers down before they restrain him. Axalte and I take turns holding each other back from running to Paltino. There are too many of them. What possible purpose could this serve? What have you done, Lute? Paltino? It all happens too fast.

The officers aren't as gentle with Paltino. They jam a Washer into his eye and flood his eye with more black than they need to, much more black than they need to. A swallowed scream chatters through my teeth. I have lost him. How many times do I have to suffer the loss of those I love? I cannot bear to see Paltino's dimply face as flat and blank as the officer I washed.

Teen Me curls up, retracts into her shell, hiding from the truth that she has lost Paltino. Axalte drapes his body around me and for the first time his beating heart, his warm breath and his honey voice do nothing for my pain.

But I know even if Teen Me doesn't. I know I get him back because he gets me back. I know this is not how the story ends. I know this is just the beginning.

The Washer that I used on the officer is still in my pocket. I pull it out. The sandstorm did not take everything. I release some black on to my fingertips and watch it writhe and evaporate like *water on a hot stone in the sun. I stare at the Washer as Lute's words repeat in my head—'what we have done can be undone'. Can be undone. I can reverse this wash.*

*This is how I will choose to remember Lute's face. Not the lost face in limbo after his reclaim, not his blank face after his wash, not his face smothered in blood and drool as he let out his last breath but his face fat with the satisfaction of knowing that he fulfilled his purpose and so he will survive . . . in spirit.*

# Chapter 17

Tied up in lace, handcuffed with jewels, I clutch on to Joyli's handheld. A 'beautiful beaded tulip-design' digs into the middle of my back at the only place I can't reach. Stuck in this frilly, lacy, beaded torture chamber of a wedding dress I have to decide who to sacrifice—Toke or the Risers?

Toke's mother's wispy voice flutters around me—'Yes, you do.' I should be more consumed by the fact that she's a Mark, but I'm not. My mind is infested with what she said to me. But I don't. I don't love Toke. I love Axalte. I have always only loved Axalte. And with that my heart, swollen with guilt, sinks through the floor. Guilt? Why guilt?

The door flies open. It's Ami, her lips pressed into a line. I slip the handheld slowly up my sleeve.

'You are my best friend. I know you, Suni. And Suni doesn't hug.' Ami charges and swipes my hands. The handheld creeps out of my sleeve and flumps on to the floor. Ami does a double take.

'You took that Hunter's handheld?' She stirs up her head again thinking it will bring her some clarity. She's so confused her shoulders bounce, her voice cracks and her feet jitter. I want to give her the peace and serenity that the truth holds—the truth that her spastic unsettled body needs. And for the first time I do what I want.

'Yes.'

'Why?' She reels in her limbs and widens her eyes.

'I am not who you think I am.'

'Are you a Riser?'

'Yes.' It feels good to say that to her. Maybe I am not doing this for her. Maybe this is for me. Maybe I need to do this to prove to myself that Teen Me is still in there, somewhere. Spunky, smart, sexy, cheeky, strong Me.

'Midnight. The kitten you asked me about. I loved it, didn't I?' Ami shields herself as if she's bracing for a hit.

'Yes.'

Ami's lips tremble into a twitchy smile. She's proud of herself. Not because she's not scared of me but because she wasn't always jittery with emptiness and she loved something once; she felt something once.

The door flies open and before I can stop her Ami picks up the handheld from the floor. It's Joyli. She rolls her shoulders back and cranes her neck as she spots her handheld . . . in Ami's hand.

'Oh, here it is! I found it. You must have dropped it by accident.' Ami shifts from one foot to another and hopscotches over to Joyli. She throws a plastic smile at me but I see the real her in her eyes—small and scared but for the first time purposeful.

'Silly me.' Joyli's face is hard. Her eyes are on Ami. She looks at her handheld and tucks it away. Ami. Why did she do that? She has no idea what she has brought on herself. I have to do something but I cannot correct her now—it will just make it worse for her.

My eyes dart around the room for something to do, something to say, and they land on Toke. Our eyes meet and he can sense it. There is something wrong.

'I guess even Legionnaires drop things every now and then. You are human after all!' Toke places his hand on Joyli's back and she softens. He looks back at me and I feign embarrassment with a downward gaze and cup my hands over each other on my stomach just as I'd imagine a pretty princess would do.

The rest of the day whizzes by in a sequence of bobbleheads, robots and zombies regurgitating recycled conversations. Ami stays with me the whole time, our arms intertwined, our fingers woven, our palms pressed together tightly. At some point she cushioned a tissue between my skin and the 'beautiful beaded tulip-design' on my back.

Toke closes the door behind the last bobblehead. Ami's hand is in mine. I don't want to let her go but I have to. She slings her once shivering body around me in a ropy hug.

'I'll see you tomorrow.' And with that she slips out. My friend. My true friend.

Now we are alone. Toke and I. Husband and wife. I hold my breath, afraid that an exhale may contain vomit. He places his hand on my shoulder and slides it up my neck until his thumb brushes my cheek.

I must look as scared on the outside as I am on the inside because he asks me if I'm okay.

'Yes, I am just tired.'

He slides his hand down my arm, settles into my hand and tugs me upstairs to the bedroom. I take short gulps of air. I can do this. I can do this. Be resourceful, Suni.

We are in his bedroom. Our bedroom? No, it's his bedroom. He plops on the bed in the usual Toke way. That would have made me chuckle under less formal circumstances. He arches his brow at me in a 'oh yeah you're here too' kinda way. I think he's just as nervous as I am. He pats the bed. It's an invitation. I can't do this. I scream inside, in my skull, in my chest until my veins bulge, throb and crawl and along my neck, temples, forehead. Paltino! Paltino! I can't do this! Do you hear me? I can't—

'Toke!' Mrs Quail weakly shrills from her distant room.

'I'm coming, Mama!' Toke springs up and out the door.

I collapse on the floor and my body wrings into a deep dry heave. I guess I haven't eaten anything since I last threw up. My hands get tangled in the frills and lace as I look around his room. Pink balloons and ribbons everywhere. I suppose he was just trying to make me feel at home, just as the plump duo Lina and Bearlett did once. But just like that room, this one too, is haunted by the hopes for someone else—the coffin of his dreamed-up non-existent bride.

A hand on my shoulder. It's Paltino. His deep dimple. My deep exhale. Malti, Snap and Doltier climb in from the window.

'You came!'

'I told you, you were not alone.' Paltino coils my strands of free hair around his finger and lets them spin out.

'Mrs Quail is a Mark,' I offer.

'I know, I asked her to distract Toke so we could get you out of here.'

'Thank you.'

'It's not what you think, sweetie pie. We have all been discovered,' Malti snaps.

'It's true. I don't know how but the Legion knows who we are and it's only a matter of time before they come after you.' Paltino pulls out the tissue, now pink with my blood, from under the lace of my dress. I hate pink. He rips the 'beautiful beaded tulip-design' in half and blows on my wound. It flashes a chill across my skin and I feel even my scalp tingle with minty relief.

'Access the database. You know you can break in now. You know how.' Snap grabs Toke's handheld from the bed and hands it to me. Malti snatches it from him.

'That's not an option,' Malti snarls. Her sharp cheeks catch the light and shroud the rest of her puckered face in darkness. She's always in hiding.

'She's right. It will be traceable to Toke,' I agree. I can't believe that Malti and I are in agreement. Judging by her unusually wide and round eyes she can't believe it either.

'Why do you care about him all of a sudden?' Malti softens.

'Just because I don't want to marry him doesn't mean I don't care about him.' Malti does not respond. I'm not sure what to make of that. 'I need to get to the mainframe in headquarters. I can access the files that way.'

'The mainframe? How the hell are we going to break into headquarters?' Snap blurts out.

'Quiet!' Paltino throws a pillow at him.

'*We* are not going to break into headquarters. *I* am. And we have no other choice. This is the only way. I won't sacrifice Toke. I won't.' Still tangled in lace I try to pull myself up. Malti stretches out her hand without looking at me. The corner of my mouth arcs in a side smile as I take her hand and rise.

'They will see us . . . you approach. Headquarters stands alone on the edge of the city. They have lookouts. We have no tunnels anywhere near it.' Clearly, Snap didn't know me before the wash. I gesture to the boys to turn around as I tear free of the lacy, frilly, ribboned torture chamber and throw on Pangean grey. I never thought I would love the feel of my crisp uniform against my skin as much as I do right now.

I tear out the dozens of pins and clips that pulled my hair into the tight bun until it falls around my shoulders.

Exhale.

'Tomorrow is Tuesday. There will be three sandstorms. We will time my entry with the first and my exit with the second.' Teen Me is in there, all right. This brings out Paltino's dimple.

Doltier clambers out of the window. Then Malti. Snap. Paltino offers me his hand as if he's asking for a dance, which I unabashedly accept. I look around the room— the pink coffin of the life I almost had. We flee out of the window as I catch a glimpse of Toke as he trots in and finds the wedding dress and *just* the wedding dress shredded in a million pieces all over the floor.

# Chapter 18

*White, shiny waves and waves and waves of layered satin crash and cover the floor. They toss muted sunlight all over the pink room to the point that Teen Me has to squint. Lina gushes at the sight of it all.*

*'It was my wedding dress.' Lina fans her eyes at a useless attempt to blow away tears. Her wedding dress floods the room with its layered breadth and sloshes about until we can no longer see the arms or chest and it becomes a gigantic pool of white satin. 'My mother gave it to me on my fifteenth birthday and so I am giving it to you on yours. Happy birthday, my beautiful Suni.' She swims through the dress and grabs me in a pillowy, mushy, squishy and comfy hug. Her ping-pong ball cheeks bounce in glee. How can I take the bounce out of those cheeks?*

*'Thank you Lina, it's perfect.'*

*'I can see you wearing this, beside Axalte, signing your wedding contracts.' Lina melts and looks at the sky as if the vision in her head is being projected up there, somewhere.*

'It will be beautiful.' Teen Me is a much better liar than me. But I am learning. Axalte bursts into the room and falls into the dress.

'Maybe this is a little big,' Lina admits with a buttery laugh.

'Suni, I found him.' Paltino. He found Paltino. I hear my blood gush through my body from my banging eardrums to my rattling kneecaps. Axalte uses the door frame as an anchor, reaches for me and pulls me out. I grab the Washer—no, now it's a Reclaimer—from the side table.

'Lina, do you need help?'

'No, Suni, I got out of this dress once. I can do it again. Well, I did have help. Bearlett!' She belly-laughs from somewhere in the satin abyss and Axalte and I hurtle out of the house and down the street.

Teen Me reversed the Washer and made the Reclaimer. The Reclaimer that the Risers have used for years to save all those people in the havens was because of Teen Me . . . was because of me.

'Are you sure it will work?' Axalte's words are broken with heavy breaths.

'It's not like I had a test subject.'

'Doesn't answer my question.'

'Yes, it does.'

Axalte stops and rests his hands on his thighs, trying to catch his breath. Sweat streams down his face. I take out a canteen of water and pass it to him. The desert sun is as relentless as Pangea today but all I can think about is Paltino. Where he is?

*Is he scared? Will this work? I don't even notice that the skin on my face has blistered red.*

'Suni! You're not wearing sunsafe?' *Axalte pulls me into the shade of an angled building and slathers my face and neck with blobs of sunsafe. He works down to my arms and with his wide, strong thumbs massages it into my skin in fluid circles.*

*He lectures me for a while. Complaining about my irresponsibility and my selfishness. He flails his large arms around, sending wafts of hot air at me. How I need to take care of myself! He runs his hand through his hair, inadvertently coating it with sunsafe and sending his now-white pokey spikes springing. How so many people need me, count on me, can't live without me, love me.*

*I look at his white boing-ing spikes and scrunched-up brow and soak up the love I have for this beautiful man. I press my sunsafed self against him and pull his lips on to mine. And in that sweaty, salty, shaded moment I catch his breath.*

'You gonna shut up now?' *I seal it with a gentle shove.*

'I'm gonna do whatever you want me to do now,' *he purrs.*

*We dash down the street as he tells me that Paltino was redistributed to East and how, to get a safe passage, he promised a border guard we would find and reclaim his sister. So, this Reclaimer better work, Suni. But we only have a few minutes left before that border guard is relieved of his post. We pick up the pace.*

*Just about everything we are doing would get us redistributed. In all my years in Pangea I never saw a wash* request for something like what we are doing. Maybe they don't wash people like us. Maybe they just kill us and wipe us from everyone's memory. They give people like us the true death— unremembered, unmourned, erased as if we never existed. We pick up the pace.

The border of North is unceremonious. No one ever comes here. No one ever tries to cross it. The border is a fifty-foot wall made of repurposed plastic. You can still see some of the original shapes of what the plastic was: water bottles, plastic bins, tricycles, a toy boat, a warped doll face. The relentless Pangean sun should melt this plastic into a river that seeps into the sand. But it doesn't. The carnivorous sun only eats flesh. This is what we did to our sun. Our source of life is also the source of death. How Pangean.

An officer flags us over to a piece of the wall that looks like it was a child's pool once: ducks wearing top hats and frogs in bowties. The Old World and its arrogance—dressing up animals in hats and booties for entertainment with one arm and skinning thousands of furry critters to tart up the elites in fluffy fur coats, scaled bags and cosy boots with the other. Animals were eaten, used, tested on, caged, starved, hunted or worn. Maybe if the Old World had shown just a little bit of humility in the face of Mother Nature, she would not have left us.

Axalte tries to speak but the shaky officer slaps his hand over Axalte's mouth and gestures for him to 'shut the hell up'. He takes out a small heat laser and cuts open a doorway and hands us the laser. He gestures 'to come back'. He slips a paper into my hand—a pencil sketch of a young girl. His sister, maybe. He puts his hand on his chest and gestures 'bring her back to me'. But from his dulled eyes I can see that he has already said his goodbyes and this request is just a tossed coin in a fountain—a wish. This better work, Suni.

We crawl through and he closes the doorway. The edges, still hot from the laser, melt together and disappear. Axalte points to East. Another wall. On the left, West. Another wall. Straight ahead another wall. South. That's it? All Pangean cities are just a few feet from each other and separated only by these walls? These fifty-foot walls of haunted garbage that we crossed so easily in just minutes? Why didn't we see this before?

It's not really these walls that hold us. These walls are just symbols. The real walls are in our minds—that don't allow us to think, that don't allow us to see, that don't allow us to leave. How do you liberate a people from the prison in their minds?

Axalte cuts through the wall to North and we slip through. The doorway melts together and disappears as my eyes burn through the sketch of the border guard's sister. I don't want to forget her face. I don't know how we can ever find her without a name, without a lead, with just a sketch and a penny wish. But if I remember her face, at least I can save her from the true death. I won't forget her face.

'You two!' an officer bellows and jogs to us. 'Have you seen a little boy? His mother can't seem to find him and she thinks he might have run this way.'

126

*We both shake our heads. Transmit, receive, process. The officer shrugs and carries on. It's those walls again. The officers rely on them. They believe that we are so imprisoned in our own minds that we are not capable of seeing and breaking through these plastic walls. It's absurd. It's arrogant. And it's worked, until now. How's that for another ridiculous irony?*

*We look at each other, wide-eyed in shock, and then we turn on our heels and speed-walk away. We trot through the streets with crooked smiles surging with the sneaky rush that breaking the law brings. We weave between tall Pangean buildings sprouting out of the ground and rows and rows of identical houses harvesting more citizens. East is just like North minus the chipfin.*

*This is it. Axalte pulls me behind a building and we watch a group of boys kick around a tumbletree. One of them jumps on another and they play-fight on the ground. Something about this play-fight looks a bit more fight and a bit less play. One of them gets over the other and punches him in the face. It's Paltino. What have they done to him?*

*'You sure this thing is going to work?' Axalte's quiet voice trembles.*

*'You already asked me that.'*

*Axalte and I skip casually over to Paltino, who pushes the other boys away, dusts off his shoulders and lopes down an alley. We pick up the pace.*

*We follow Paltino until we are in the narrow, shaded, deep alley alone. Just the three of us.*

'This is not going to be easy. He's going to resist,' I warn Axalte. Paltino swings around. His face, hardened and worn, has lost its glimmer. Axalte pounces on him and Paltino crumbles under Axalte's strength.

'Stop!' Paltino screams and Axalte clamps his hand on Paltino's mouth.

'Hurry up, Suni, before someone hears!' Axalte whisper-yells.

I dive between them and place the Reclaimer on Paltino's forehead. He squirms an arm free of Axalte's hold and slaps the Reclaimer from my hand. It smashes into a rock. Axalte gets distracted for a moment and releases his hand from Paltino's mouth.

'Stop it, Suni!' Paltino blurts. We freeze. How does he remember who I am? 'Because I am a Mark. And my Mark is that I can't be washed.' Paltino frees himself of Axalte's hold.

'Why didn't you tell us you couldn't be washed?' Axalte backs off.

'I obviously didn't know until they tried to wash me.' Paltino spits out some dirt that flew into his mouth during the scuffle.

'Then why did you come out here and let them turn you into this? Why didn't you come back?' I ask.

'Because I had to pretend I was washed. Otherwise I would have revealed myself as a Mark. I am just a few weeks away from becoming an officer and then I will be authorized to travel between cities.' Hide in plain sight. I pull him into me and let myself go in the warmth of his arms. Axalte snatches us both up in a huge woody embrace.

'What did I just break?' Paltino thumbs his chin bristles.

'A Reclaimer. Suni did it. She really did it.' My oaky man is proud of me.

'As long as there are stars in the sky what has been done can be undone,' I say, knowing this will bring out his dimple. It does.

'Lute?' Paltino asks with his whole face.

'Not yet, Paltino. But we will find him.' I grab his hand. He nods.

'Can you make more?'

'Yes. But I need Washers and they have heightened security at the Academy now.'

'Don't worry. I will get you all the Washers that you need.'

# Chapter 19

At the mouth of the tunnel Paltino shoves things into my pockets: a knife, water, helder leaves, kierry berry, encryption chips, a small laser, a Reclaimer. I chuckle at the Reclaimer. It's a cocky chuckle. It's a well-deserved cocky chuckle.

'We improved on your design a bit.' Paltino is not boasting; he's apologetic, again.

'Every memory that comes back to me you are also going to hear?' I ask but I know the answer.

'Yes.'

'So I'm like an open book here?' He shrugs. Nice. 'You're still annoying. Just so you know.' I wrinkle my lips and poke him in the shoulder a few times until I get that dimple back. There it is.

'That girl in the sketch. Did we find her?' Paltino continues stuffing my pockets. He can't answer that, I guess. 'Okay, well, did you find her after I was taken?'

'No. Most of the time people don't get . . . what they want.' The weight of that truth cracks his voice at the end. Dimple is gone.

'You're seriously hardcore for doing this.' Snap pats me on the back. Malti does not sneer at me. Which is tantamount to a hug for Malti. I kinda like her fire.

Paltino keeps shoving stuff in my pockets: isotrope code, a snack. A snack?

'It could take a while.' He pushes it in my pocket. I pull it out and chuck it at him.

'I am not going to fit in the vents with all this stuff you're loading me with. But thanks anyway, *Dad*.' I kiss his cheek with more comfort than I should have, drape myself in an opaque plastic sheet and disappear into the sandstorm. From little cave monster to plastic ghost.

The sandstorm disguises me, but it blinds me as well. I keep thinking of Pangean Me's voice repeating 'you don't ever go into sandstorms, you don't ever go into sandstorms' like a mantra. I can only see inches in front of my face—nothing beyond the plastic. I push hard forward with each sinking footstep. With each breath I suck the plastic into my mouth and have to use the little air in my lungs to blow it out. The sand beats me from every direction and with heavy fists the hot winds punch, slap and push me down. I struggle to hold on to the plastic and keep moving. Just keep moving. I fight it. Fight it. Just a little more and my foot hits the external wall of the building.

I tuck the plastic into my waistband and press my hands against the wall. Through the plastic I feel along the wall for the vent. I scuff my feet to the right and stumble. A gust of air rips the plastic from me and there I stand, a little speck in the giant churning, moaning, roaring, monster of a storm. This is not nature. This is us. We have done this. We have created this. We have turned nature into a vengeful, spiteful, murderous and unholy beast. Unnatural nature. The mother of all ironies.

I squeeze my eyes and mouth shut. I can't breathe. Each breath is just sand burning my nostrils, biting at my skin, cheeks, neck. I run my hands along the wall, faster.

I can't hold my breath for much longer. I need to get in. Now. I stretch up and pull my sinking feet up to the left, faster, faster. My left hand catches on the ridges of a vent. The vent. I push my fingers through the grate and pull. Nothing.

I can't open my eyes—the sand whips my face. I press my mouth up to the grate and gulp in as much clean air as I can. I feel in my pocket and pull out the laser. I cut through the grate and pull my body through the hole, slicing my leg on the raw edge. I suck in as much air as my lungs will take. Keep sucking and gulping air, keep gulping and sucking until my chest slows and I breathe again.

Sand is in my ears, eyes, nose, mouth, hair. The more I wipe the more appears, as if it's pouring on me from above. I blink as much as I can from my eyes and examine my wound. I can't keep them open for more than a few seconds before the sand begins to grind through my tears. In quick glances I see the gash is not deep but it is bleeding. The last thing I want to do is leave a trail of blood leading straight to me. I tear off my sleeve but the vent is too narrow so I can't tie it around my leg.

I can almost hear Paltino's whiny voice saying 'use the helder leaves'. I pull them out and put them in my mouth to dampen them. No saliva. I pull out the water, flush out my eyes and rinse my mouth, spitting out as much sand as I can. I spend the next minute sucking the roof of my mouth with my tongue, trying to get as much spit as I can while trying to ignore the few granules of sand scratching up the inside of my mouth. Eureka, saliva. I jam the leaves in my mouth and stretch my arm as long as the walls of the vent will allow to place them on my wound. I watch my blood seep into the leaves and pull them into the wound like glue. Okay, Paltino, happy?

I slide through the narrow vent. My shoes clunk and the sound echoes until it barrels through the vents. I curl up, trying to stop the steel vents from clanging in the vibrations but I can't stop them. I just hold still until the vibration slows.

My fingers and palms are too slippery with spit-up sand to pull myself through. I slip off my shoes and press my toes quietly on the cool steel to slide forward inch by inch by inch by inch like a limbless chipfin. I have to pass four vents. One. Toes to steel. Two. Stretch. Arch. Flex. Toes to steel. Three. A group of officers swarm in the room below, packing their weapons, talking about the cute girl with the legs on the seventh floor. Toes to steel. Four.

I peer through the grates of the vent and watch one woman change into her uniform. She puckers at her reflection and half-turns her body to see how her butt looks and leaves. The things the zombies worry about. She wears no identification. Arrogance. The same arrogance that let Axalte and me cross the walls into North.

I slide the grate up and jump down. My leg buckles under the fall and I slam into the plastic bench. I'm more hurt than I realized. I just have a few minutes, maybe even seconds, before someone enters. Looking like this, covered in sand, identification or not, I will be found.

I open a locker, nothing. Another, nothing. A third— jackpot! A Pangean uniform. I shower, careful to make sure that every grain of sand and drop of blood goes down the drain. I swathe my leg in fresh helder leaves and tie it up tight with a torn towel. It's bleeding. I slip into the uniform that's too big but not big enough to draw attention. And my shoes—they should work. I brush my wet hair and weave it into Pangean Suni's tight, tugging, snaking braid. The uniform has no pockets but I tuck one of the encrypted chips in my braid. I reweave the braid tighter. This time it is hiding something. I bundle up my clothes and all remnants of me, swaddle them in a towel and shove them into the bottom of a trash bin.

I stare at that bundle. I don't have anything other than that chip. Will I need any of that stuff Paltino jammed in my pockets? The Reclaimer. I should take the Reclaimer. I hear voices chirp by the door. No time. I shove my hand into the bundle and pull out the Reclaimer.

Two women enter. I slip the Reclaimer up into my sleeve. They look at me, a little perplexed. They are looking at my sleeve. They know.

I glance down. My fingertips glisten red. Am I bleeding? No, it's kierry berry. I must have burst them when I reached in for the Reclaimer. That's why they are staring.

Find my inner bobblehead. I pucker my lips at my reflection, smear my lips with the kierry berry and half-turn to check out my butt.

'Want some?' I offer up my hand, hoping they don't notice it tremble.

'No thanks!' they bubble in unison.

I rinse off the remainder in the sink, dry my hands and strut by them, swaying my hips with each step and letting my braid wag like a tail.

'Good day, ladies.'

'Good day.' They bought it!

I dip my head to them and walk out quickly but casually into a wide tunnel filled with officers and Pangean workers. Everyone is hustling and bustling with papers and their washed purpose. Everyone knows what they're doing here and where they are going, everyone except me. If I look confused they will know I don't belong here. I follow the traffic down the hall until everyone disappears into doorways and I am at a dead end.

My breath quickens—if anyone sees me at the dead end they will realize that I don't belong here. I spin around and walk the other way, following another flock until they all disappear behind closed doors. I don't see any stations or any terminals where I can do this. Where am I supposed to go?

I spin around again and tack behind another flock. This one enters into an elevator and everyone presses a separate floor as they enter. I squeeze into the back of the elevator. They all turn to me with their blank faces and tilt their heads in unison. I didn't press an elevator floor. I push through the flock and select the only floor not chosen—the fifth. I press the button and shrink to the back of the elevator. Some eyes move away from me and some don't. A voice fills the elevator.

'Clearance?' A plasma keyboard appears. The flock herds me to the front of the elevator. I have to enter a code. This didn't happen for anyone else. Now I know why that floor wasn't pushed. It's too late to backtrack. Everyone in the elevator glares at me. I can feel their breath on the back of my neck. Why would I need higher clearance if I'm in an Expert uniform? There is nothing higher than an

Expert. No, there *was* nothing higher than an Expert and the very thing that I am here for is the very thing that is going to get me in. I type: LEGION.

'Name?' the voice demands. I type: Joyli. I don't even know her last name anymore. This is not going to work.

'Password?' Does that mean it worked? I don't know this. I can't guess this. Not on the first try and if I don't I'm done for. A cluster of officers stomp through the hallways just outside the open elevator doors. I glance at the Pangean to my right—a young boy of maybe sixteen or seventeen. He clenches and unclenches his white knuckled hand, his nails chewed down to slivers. His eyes are not on me. He's hiding something too. Not him.

I glance at the Pangean on my left—an older woman, maybe twenty-five or thirty? She whistles her breath through her thin, pointy nose as she glares at me with a programmed anger. She's probably a mother; she's just as innocent and she doesn't deserve this. But I have no time and I have no choice.

'Riser!' I bellow at the stomping officers and dive on to the older woman as I slip the Reclaimer out of my sleeve and into her refusing hand. I heave her on top of me; she wriggles to free herself but the more she moves, the harder she's ensnared in the trap. Before anyone can tell who is doing what, the officers rip her off me and the Reclaimer slides out of her hand. That's all they needed.

'Riser scum!' an officer spits. Pangeans hiss and bark at her as the officers drag her out of the elevator and down the hall by her hair. The Pangeans snarl after them as that young officer with the chewed nails uses the distraction to slip away. I think she screams and pleads. But I don't hear it. I can't. All I can hear is the gurgles of guilt boil up my throat, flood my head and singe the back of my eyes.

I traded her life for mine. No, I traded her life for all Risers. This was not for me. This was for The Uprising, one life for many. I want to believe that. I have to believe that. But my comfort is making me uncomfortable and I notice that the elevator is empty as the sugary voice repeats.

'Password?'

The angry Pangean mob is just a few feet ahead of me. I have to do this. That woman bought me a minute. Think. What would Joyli choose as a password? This new Joyli? She's a monster. All I know about her is that she is a bloodthirsty hunter. Hunter. That's it!

I type: Hunter.

'Access denied. Password?' That's not it! A Pangean throws a glance at me and quickly goes back to the snarls and hisses of the mob. I don't have time for this. I have to think. What did we talk about? Hunters. Her marriage. Her husband. The Commander. Yes, that has to be it.

I type: Commander.

'Access denied. Password?' I can't do this. The Pangeans begin to rustle, having lost the passion to follow the mob.

They straighten up, one by one. They are going to come back into the elevator. If I don't have this password then I am finished. The Risers are finished. And everything was for nothing. I try not to look at the woman's limp body in the middle of the dissipating Pangean mob. I can't let that happen. But, I don't know her. I don't know this new Joyli. How am I supposed to know what she would choose as her password?

Be resourceful, Suni.

Maybe pieces of the real Joyli are in there somewhere, just like pieces of the real me were surfacing in the sleepy, lonely hours of the night. Maybe. The Pangeans slowly meander back into the elevator behind me, wiping the spit from their mouths, straightening their uniforms and smoothing their hair. This is the last chance I have.

I type: Ballerina.

An alarm bell sounds. I'm done. I have been caught and now there is no hope for the Risers. I tighten my fists, ready to go out with whatever fight I have in me.

'Please exit the elevator. There is a Legionnaire onboard. Thank you for your cooperation.' The sugary voice commands the robots and zombies to leave. Transmit, receive, process, and with apologies and a lot of head bowing they are out. I did it?

A sickening relief washes over me, relieved that I have not been found, that the Risers have a chance, that that woman didn't get washed for nothing, that the real Joyli is still in Joyli somewhere and sickened by the fact that I sacrificed that woman, that Joyli will never know why she chose that password and that deep inside, above all else, I am very proud of myself right now.

'Legionnaire, in the future, please feel free to access your private elevators in the south bank if you prefer,' the voice offers in the softest way a computerized voice can.

'Thank you.' As the elevator zips up I have to forcefully hold in a breaking smile.

'Fifth floor. Have a nice day, Legionnaire, and thank you for your service to The People.' I step off the elevator and into the empty and dark fifth floor. With each step the lights illuminate around me—just like a spotlight.

'Legionnaire. Welcome to the headquarters of East. We have been anticipating the arrival of the Legion. I am pleased to welcome you as our first Legionnaire. We were expecting the Commander. However, we are most pleased to meet you. Is there anything I can help you with today?' It's the system. An accusation coated in a sugary voice. I don't have that much time.

'The Commander has sent me on a special assignment. I need access to a terminal.' I have to sound official. I am now in the belly of the beast.

'Of course, Legionnaire.' The system illuminates a terminal on the other side of the hall. As I walk to the terminal only the pathway on which I walk is illuminated.

As if the system is purposefully hiding the contents of this floor from me. I casually look into the grey area on my right. It's filled with rows and rows of shelves stocked with boxes labelled with doses. It's medication. Medication is illegal in Pangea. Maybe they hold contraband here? Why would they do that? Why wouldn't they destroy it?

I reach the terminal and open Joyli's file. Not a Mark. Legion. Five numbers are listed in the Legion. That means there are only five Legionnaires. Acquired Gifts Test Results. Catches my eye. I select it:

1. Teleportation: three uses per dose. Each one less effective than the previous.

2. Psycho-electrocution: Effective for six-hour period. Unlimited usage.

3. Derma Scald: Effective for six-hour period. Unlimited usage.

4. Changeling: three uses per dose. Each change lasts one hour.

5. Speed: Effective for six-hour period in twenty-minute bursts. Unlimited usage.

6. Connection: Effective for six-hour period. Unlimited usage.

7. No two gifts can be used simultaneously.

8. All gifts can only be received by those who hold the gene.

9. All attempts to administer gifts to those without the gene have resulted in fatalities.

What are doses? What is the gene? Have they found a way to manufacture Marks? Is that what they call Gifts?

'Legionnaire, why are you accessing your own files?' The system should not be asking me questions like that. It knows. I don't have much time. I try to open a hyperlink to 'Memory Acquisition Results' when I see my face flash on all the plasmas with the word RISER stamped across it.

'I ran your fingerprints from the keyboard, Suni Tygyr. Surrender, Riser, there is no escape,' the system warns. I pull out the encrypted chip from my braid and load it into the terminal. The plasmas go blank and the virus corrupts the system, mutating her voice until she has none.

Without the system controlling anything all the lights turn on in the floor. I dart over to the aisles of medication and search the labels until I find it. I grab a few boxes and bolt for the steps. I half-trip half-bolt down one flight, hearing officers' voices nearing from the top and bottom like a tightening noose. I open the door and throw myself into the fourth floor. There are large prodding machines looming over empty exam tables. Thick straps and buckles hang from the tables. They are restraints. This looks like the labs during the Sterilizations. The labs filled with Seggies being experimented on. The labs that led to The Cleanse. The walls are lined with syringes filled with different colours. An officer rounds the corner and freezes as he sees me.

He's tall. Must be at least six feet, and his hands are so big they could lash around my neck twice and snap it like a plastic twig. And he's got a large gun—and it's not a stunray. I lunge at the gun and he slams me against the wall. We both clutch his gun and I push the nozzle with all the force of my body towards him as he pushes the nozzle towards me. He's stronger than me. The nozzle nears my shoulder and we are so close to each other I can feel the heat of his breath. I can't fight him, not physically. A droplet of sweat rolls off his nose and into my mouth. My mouth.

I press my lips, still wet with kierry berry, on to his until his unwilling lips soften under mine. I snap the gun out of his hand but I no longer need it. His body wilts and I catch him. He heaves for a breath and I notice for the first time how young he is. He is just a little boy with a gun. I hold him for the whole minute that the kierry berry takes to eat away at him and then he's gone.

I killed two people today, two innocent people.

Boots thump behind me. I can't let them die for nothing. I haul his body into the stairwell, grab the boxes and slip into the nearest room—a room full of coffins. I hide behind a tall cabinet and peek through a narrow sliver to the lab. The wall of coloured syringes is labelled 'Acquired Gifts'. Those are the gifts I just read about on the terminal. Joyli had psycho-electrocution. That's what she used on Fellie. These must be the doses that Legionnaires take to get the powers they have. Joyli must have had the gene, the gene that would make her a Legionnaire, one of only five. That's why they took her. The officers appear around the corner. They are in no particular hurry and don't look like they are looking for me but they are coming into this room. I look around for somewhere to hide—nothing but coffins.

I slide over to the first coffin and slowly pry it open, hoping that it's empty. It's not. I don't look at the contents long enough to see what or who it is. Just knowing there is a body inside is horrible enough. I slip in, lying down on the cold, stiff body, and hold the coffin open a crack to let in air and a shred of light. It smells like stale rot. I try to breathe only through my mouth. The officers enter the room.

'Of course, Jut leaves these for us to take out.' One officer grabs a power drill from the wall and walks over to the coffin. He pushes the lid closed and drills it, shutting me in the dark, airless coffin lying on a corpse. Paltino! Paltino!

Just relax, don't waste air. Paltino will find me. He will come for me. He knows where I am—he's been watching, listening. Just stay calm and save your air.

For the next few moments I swallow screams and rock back and forth in the coffin as I am carried away. A big drop thrusts me into the corpse. Its rigid arms pin me and its cold, hard cheek presses against mine. It's a girl. It was a girl and her hair falls into my mouth.

Pitter-patter. Like it's raining on the coffin. Good. Acid rain will burn right through and then I can run out. I start gulping in air knowing I'm about to get out. Until the pitter-patter deepens with thuds and I realize it's not rain falling on the coffin . . . . it's sand.

I am being buried alive.

'Paltino! Paltino!'

# Chapter 20

'Paltino! Paltino!' Teen Me pounds on a door. My hair floats around me—almost in a delay—as I grab a nearby chair and smash it against the door. Again. Again. Until the door swings open and Paltino, fully adorned in an officer's uniform, frowns at me.

'What for The People's sake are you doing?' Paltino throws his hands in the air to shield himself from the airborne chair bits.

'Paltino? You're okay?'

'Of course I'm okay. I just wanted some privacy. Thanks for that.' Paltino slumps on the edge of the bed. The room is the typical Pangean bedroom. Cold, grey and empty. This isn't Paltino's bedroom. It's his caseworker's assignment. In the corner of the room his washed caseworker, whom Paltino was assigned to protect, blankly sways and periodically bumps into the washed case, a sunny teen girl, whom the caseworker was assigned to wash today. By the looks of it the caseworker did his job. This is how Paltino buys time to build the resistance—washing his coworker. Poor guy has been washed so many times we have no idea what would happen if we tried to reclaim him. He's got so much black in his skull sometimes I think his head will burst. But every time Paltino tries to bring him on our side he refuses and then Paltino washes him again. I guess in some form of twisted logic it's kinda his own fault.

'You just stormed out with that crazy look you get and I didn't know what you were going to do. I mean you can't just do that. You're armed now.' I slump next to him on the bed and nudge his shoulder with mine. 'Did you just say for The People's sake?' I chuckle.

'I am spending too much time in this uniform. It's been weeks since I have been an officer, months since they took Lute and we still can't find him.'

'I know, look, I am graduating next week and with my scores they will assign me to the mainframe. I know it. Then I will find him. I promise.'

He just shakes his head and protests for a while, his voice stained with hopelessness. His eyes keep going to the twine ring on my finger. My engagement ring.

'I love you, Suni.'

'I love you too, Paltino.'

'No, I love you, Suni.' His eyes meet mine and redden with pain. It's not just Lute. It's this ring. It's the engagement. It's me. I have done this to him.

The caseworker bumps into the wall and falls backwards on to the floor. We both watch him slither around, unable to get up, unable to turn over, just stuck for no apparent reason at all.

*I put my hand on Paltino's face and turn him to me. I caress his flat cheek and trace where his dimple should be. I want to take this pain away from him. I want to soothe him and protect him as he has done for me for years. I am so disgusted that I did this to him. To my friend, to my best friend.*

'We would have been great together. In another life.' He spins the ring on my finger.

*I pull away from him. Maybe he needs me to go. He slaps on a plastic smile and scoops up the caseworker, plopping him in a chair. He scurries about picking up the pieces of the chair I all but shattered.*

'I better wake him up soon. It's getting harder and harder to invent memories to replace the time I steal from him. I don't think I'm creative enough. At the very least I should give him some good fake memories. But the ones I give him are probably just as boring as life is.' He shoves his hands deep in his pockets and flashes his dimple. It's shallower than it should be and his eyes have lost their light.

*I dimmed his light. Teen Me is only Me, after all.*

# Chapter 21

I choke on the realization that this coffin might be mine. I scream and kick the corpse off me. I don't even care if the officers hear me . . . I just want to get out of this darkness. The harder I kick it off the harder the cold stiff body slams into me. In the dark our limbs twist together and the more I squirm and wriggle the more we tangle. I shriek in the fear that we may remain intertwined in this dark box in the ground for eternity.

The wood grinds and splinters. I pound on the door and push with every cell in my body. The door flies open. It's Paltino. He reaches into the grave and pulls me into his arms. I bury my face in his chest. The warmth of his skin feels better than the oxygen in my lungs. He wraps his arms around me and holds me. I know we should run, we don't have time, I know we need to go but I can't let go and he doesn't make me. He lets me heal in his arms until I am ready.

I am ready. I pull the boxes of medicine from the coffin. The corpse lies face down. I stare at her grey dress stained with blood. Her limbs that crushed my chest like boulders are just as frail as tumbletree twigs. She had no one to come for her. No one to open her door. Alone in life. Alone in death.

I gently turn her over. If I see her face they cannot erase her. She will exist somewhere even if it's just in my memory. All I can do for her, as all I could do for the sketch girl is save her from a true death. Paltino looks away. With a loud clunk I flip her on to her back. When I see her face I feel those heavy lead anchors stitched into my gut pull down—guilt.

It's Fellie.

I step back, tripping over the bodies of the two officers that buried me. Paltino scoops me up. Officers approaching. Now we have to run. And we do . . . into the twisting tunnels and caves. Running. Running.

Paltino pulls me to a stop. I don't want to stop. If we stop I will have to think about Fellie. About how I failed her. How it's my fault that her baby is dead. How it's my fault that *she* is dead. I didn't come for her. No one came for her. I failed her. How can I carry this—it's too heavy and it eats away at my insides like acid rain.

I can hear her words. 'Own my pain. Own your pain.' I'm trying, Fellie. I am trying. Paltino fiddles around with my leg wound.

'We have to get to the Riser meet.'

'Not yet, I have to do something first.'

'Suni, we can't go into Pangea right now; it's too dangerous.' I ignore him and start running again. I know my way through these tunnels. I designed them. Even with my bloodied leg Paltino trails behind me. Own my pain. Own my pain.

* * *

'Suni, this is a bad idea.' I pause at Toke's bedroom window. Still dressed in his wedding suit he lies—no splays—on his side, shoes and everything. The shredded wedding dress bits whir in the slight breeze the open window carries in. He didn't even close the window. He wasn't washed to love me. He just loved me. That was his misfortune. This may be a bad idea but I won't leave him like this, alone and broken. He's not alone. I want him to know that.

I slip in through the open window and stare down at him in the bed. Toke, the spit-shined, badge-wearing, principle-tattooed, puff-chested Pangean dreamboat has been reduced to an empty shell. I won't dim the lights of his eyes too.

I place the boxes of medicine on the bed. Antibiotics. Mrs Quail is not going to die. Toke will not be alone. I know this cannot make up for what I have done to him. It's really not about making amends. It's not about what he thinks about me or whether he forgives me. Apologies are self-serving and explanations are excuses. His forgiveness will only soothe my soul. I'm not interested in being soothed. I just don't want him to be alone. I don't want him to feel lost, empty or betrayed. He's in the dark of the coffin and he needs someone to open the door. It doesn't matter what he thinks of me. I just need him to know he will always have someone to open the door.

He rises up on his elbows and looks at me over his shoulder. His eyebrows dip at the ends. His face looks like he's asking a question but he's silent. Paltino pulls out a weapon and I shoo him away. Toke lazily glances at Paltino then back at me. Toke could take both of us down before we even blinked but I know he won't do that. The Pangean officer who lives and dies by the rules was so much more than I ever gave him credit for. He looks at the boxes of medicine and turns back around, coiling into himself.

I walk over to him and slowly bend to him. I press my lips against his forehead.

'In another life,' I whisper in his ear. He does not move to watch me slip out of the window. But as Paltino leads me through the darkness, away from scouring officers and into the slim protection of nearby shadows I realize that Mrs Quail was right. I do love Toke.

'Suni, I don't think we should risk it and try to make it to the meet. We will stay in the tunnels tonight.' No, Paltino. I know where we can go. No point actually speaking. I know he is listening to everything I think and right now the less sound we make the better.

I like that he hears me. These thoughts are not secrets I wish to hold inside me. They are the poisoned fruits of my pain. Maybe knowing that he's with me, inside my messed-up head, gives me some strength. No other can know me as he does. There are no masks we wear, no plastic smiles, no sweet lies to dull the sharp edge of truth. Poor Paltino's trapped in the bitterness of my mind. He lifts my hand to his lips as if to disagree.

We have reached Ami's house. Paltino yanks my arm and pulls me behind a small rock. A blue light flashes from Ami's room. It's Joyli. She's in Ami's room. Her eyes flash with blue lightning. That's Buzz's Mark. Joyli has Buzz's Mark.

Ami stands before Joyli, unmoved. She just stands there. Why isn't she running? This is because of the handheld. It's because she grabbed the handheld from the floor at the wedding so Joyli thinks she took it. Why did she do that? I took it! It was me!

Paltino grabs me by the waist and muffles my mouth with his hand.

'You can't reveal yourself now. We are not ready. If we do it this way, they will get you and everything we have done will go to waste. Everyone we have lost will be for nothing. Nothing. She picked up that handheld because it was her purpose. She knew it. She knows it now.' Paltino tightens his grip on my body as I kick and fight him.

Joyli puts her hand on Ami's shoulder and shards of blue lightning spark out of her body and slice through the air and into Ami. Ami's body shakes and convulses as the shards slice through her, electrocuting her again and again. Tears pour from the corners of my eyes and my body goes limp in Paltino's grip as his hold turns to an embrace. Ami is gone. She is gone. Gone.

# Chapter 22

*'Isn't this a bit dramatic?' Teen Me's voice in a black room. I hope I am talking to someone. My elbows, knees and back bump into structures, shelves maybe? Tight dark box.*

*A lightbulb dangling inches from my forehead flickers on. It's Teen Me and Paltino in a closet in the headquarters. Both of us sport Pangean officer uniforms and dodge the occasional cleaning supplies that slide off the shelf and on to our heads.*

*'Sorry, all the conference rooms were booked.' Oh, look at Paltino being cheeky. 'Look, you dragged me out here to East. You know I hate it here. What is it?' With every inhale my chest presses against his. I try to move in another direction and the curve of my hip pushes into his thigh. He fumbles trying to find a place for his hands—a place not on me. I chuckle at the absurdity until I realize the chill of my indifference. Our wriggling bodies pressed against each other in this dark place locked away from the world is funny to me but to Paltino it's—if he believed in such a thing—hell. 'Let's not waste time.'*

*'I found him.'*

'Suni, then what are we doing here? Let's go get him.'

'It's not that simple, Paltino. He's been under for a year. There are other . . .' I stumble for the right word. I never stumble. 'Considerations.' The lightbulb dangles between us, highlighting the shadows under his eyes. The year has cost him.

'Are you saying you can't reclaim him?'

'In theory, yes I can. But that's not what I am talking about. He was washed into a marriage.'

'Okay, we will reclaim her too. I don't see the problem.'

'There's more.' His eyes droop in the corners now like teardrops. It's the weight of his loss wearing his skin down. Lute is not Paltino's real brother. Like all Pangeans, they were redistributed as infants. They never knew their real parents and they never met their real siblings. Except for me, of course. I had them and then I lost them. And now all I have is memories and gaping holes in my heart. Well, Teen Me had the memories. Pangean Me just had the holes.

This pull between Paltino and Lute is not biological. It's not their shared blood, lineage or DNA. It's an emotional connection—built on a different plane. It's the basis of the theory of redistribution: to ensure that we love all children as our own, all infants will be taken within one hour of their birth and exchanged with another newborn infant. We will love all children as our own because they may just be our own. We will love all people like brothers and sisters because they may just be our brothers and sisters. Families are a hodgepodge of genes, a patchwork of beings thrown together randomly by The People.

*But we do love our forged families even without being washed. Paltino loves Lute as much as I love my sweet baby brother Hayk. And even though I am crippled by my hollowed heart, I do love Lina and Bearlett. This is how much we need to belong somewhere, belong to someone, belong to something even if it was chosen for us. Even if it's fake and even if we know it's fake.*

*Like the scar on my hand from the acid rain, from the burn that Fellie soothed with live helder, the wash has become a part of me, an ugly, itchy, permanent part of me. At some point, the wash becomes real. And who you were during your wash becomes an ugly, itchy battle scar on who you will always be. Reclaimed Me knows that but Teen Me hasn't learned that, yet.*

*Paltino is not going to understand why we can't reclaim Lute right now. I have to show him. Regardless of how much this will hurt him he has to see it to understand why Lute cannot see it.*

*The pocket zipper on my leg catches his pant, pulling my leg into his. The more I try to pull it back the more we slip into each other. I try not to look at him. Not because I'm uncomfortable but because I know he is. Paltino slides his hand down my leg and tears his pant-leg free. Even in this faint buzzing dangling light I can see his cheeks flush.*

*'Come with me.' I crack the door open and wait for a hoard of officers to stomp around a corner. I leave our little box; Paltino follows. Stone-faced, straight-backed, chins lifted, we click-clack down the hall into the stairwell. Teen Me has clickity-clackety*

shoes, not thumping boots. The shoes of a mainframe Expert who works in the headquarters, not the laced-up boots of the labouring officer. And again I am proud of and maybe a little oddly envious of Teen Me.

A few flights of stairs. Winding hallway. Doorway. Is that an officer following us? Narrow passage. Another flight of stairs. He's gone; no one is behind us. Doorway. The Empty Room.

That's what they call it. The 'Empty Room'. But it's not empty—it's never empty. It's where they hold the dead before they are buried. We don't really ask how they died. We just assume they all died of natural causes. Or at least we used to.

Pangeans don't bury their own. Deaths are registered with The People and then officers bring the bodies to the Empty Room where other officers bury the dead at unmarked undisclosed locations. No ceremonies, no graves, nothing. Funerals encourage excessive mourning that scares The People. Too much emotion makes people think or not think. Either way it makes people unpredictable. The People don't like unpredictability. And there we have it. Every Pangean principle boils down to another way for The People to control us. The People. We are supposed to be The People. The People are supposed to be all of us, united. How can we oppress ourselves? The logic is twisted and circular. A beast eating its own tail. Another ridiculous irony.

'Is he dead?' Paltino's face drops further.

I shake my head and point him towards a cot in the corner. A tiny lump draped in flowing plastic, smooth as silk but for a sharp peak—a nose. A baby. Paltino does not move closer and *he does not turn to ask me why I have brought him here. A lot is said by his silence. The rest I say in my mind, as if doing so will dull its edge.*

*She was a baby girl just a few hours old, born a Mark. A strong Mark. She revealed herself to the officer who picked her up for redistribution in front of her parents. They knew what her fate would be. They tried to fight the officer but they couldn't overpower him. The officer took the baby and washed her parents off her memory as if she never existed, erased her. And here she lies in her true death.*

*Paltino does not move. His feet are planted firmly, his fists clenched, his cheeks pumped with air as if he is bracing for a tidal wave.*

*We cannot reclaim Lute right now. He will refuse to hide in plain sight. He will not be able to function in Pangea and fulfill his assigned role. He will expose himself, his wife and possibly you. He will be unable to control his fury. No one would be able to. We can only reclaim him once we have created a place where we can take him. A place we can let him grieve. A place that is safe—a haven.*

*'This is his daughter.' Paltino says the words that I could not.*

*'Yes.'*

*'What was her name?'*

*'They had not named her yet.' Paltino pulls the plastic down, exposing her face. Curled eyelashes line large 'U' eyelids, a round head with a centred patch of chocolatey hair, her moonlight-red top lip dips over the bottom as if the bottom lip is sucked in—just*

*like Lute's. Her skin glows in shades of pinks so she just looks like she's sleeping.*

*Paltino thumbs her pudgy cheek. He kisses her forehead.*

'Una. Her name is Una. Una's not gone. She's not gone. Not gone.'

# Chapter 23

Paltino holds on to my arm and pulls me through miles of dark winding tunnels. Running. I don't even feel my feet on the ground, my breath quickening, my limbs thrashing into the jagged-edged walls, nothing. It's as if I'm just a feather trailing behind him, weightless, floating in total surrender. I killed Ami.

I washed Joyli. I could have given her the extra week she asked for. I could have let her run. I could have shown her Teen Me—the smart, cheeky, strong and just Teen Me. The Me that would have warned her that we were coming. The Me that would have spent the year teaching her the tunnels, showing her Una and giving her choices. The Me that would have saved her.

But I didn't. I left her with Pangean Suni—the brittle, scared, weak, achy Me. The Me that spent the year finding her suitors. The Me that valued Toke's place in The People over her right to choose her life. The Me that washed her. The Me that gave her to The People blank and empty. Look at her now. Look what I made her into.

I killed Ami.

Paltino reels me in and I wilt against his chest humming with his sweet words that I cannot even hear. I close my eyes and slip into the dark gluey pools of guilt, regret and pain. I just want to stay in here. In the stickiness of my mistakes.

Fellie's words. 'Own my pain, own your pain.' Am I going to be the Pangean Me and let this break me? Or am I going to be Teen Me and let this make me?

I pull away from Paltino. At some point we must have emerged from the tunnels. Lights from the four cities twinkle above the walls in the distance beyond what looks like miles of red moonlit desert sand. But it can't be miles . . . we could not have run that far. How long did I lose myself in the dark places of my mind?

We are huddled in the curved branches of a trio of trees. Real rooted trees coated in thick, rough bark with wide, strong branches like Axalte's arms.

'Where is he?' I know Paltino is listening in.

'I don't know.'

'Is he dead?'

'I don't know.'

We weave our hands together, both hit hard by the thought and we quickly change the topic.

'What Joyli did . . .' He doesn't want to say it. As if his word choice makes this any better or could make it any worse. 'The power she used was just like Buzz's. It was psycho-electrocution.'

'I take it that's not particularly common?'

'Never seen anyone beside Buzz with it. Until Joyli.'

'And the power she used that night in Una, on Fellie was just like Flora's.'

'Are you sure?'

'Yes, you don't think that's what those syringes were in headquarters? What did they call them—"Acquired Gifts"?'

'I wrote them down as you read them.' We release each other's hands as Paltino pulls out a folded paper and scrunches his brow as he reads it. His heavy eyes dart from side to side. He chews on his lower lip and periodically rubs his eyes with closed fists like a sleepy toddler. 'Yes, number two, psycho-electrocution. Buzz's power. Effective for a six-hour period. Unlimited usage. And number three, derma scald. Flora's power. Also effective for a six-hour period. Unlimited usage.'

We both lock our eyes together and as if I can read his mind too, I know we've both come to the same realization. The People have discovered how to harness a Mark's power. That's what those syringes were—doses. And The People have been administering these doses to the Legion. That's why they have the powers that they do.

They are invincible. Toke. If they went after Ami they are going to go after Toke.

'Malti is with him. She will keep him safe.'

'Malti? She may kill him just to piss me off.'

'Don't be so hard on her. She was just always protective of Toke. He's her brother. She tried to reclaim him but he's been under too long. The reclaim just didn't take. It was really messy. The caseworker was particularly difficult. We had to . . . well, it was messy.'

'The Riser that Toke met, the one that killed the last caseworker he was assigned to protect is Malti? His sister?' I can't imagine what that was like for her. To be face-to-face with her brother whom she loved and all he wanted to do was kill her. If that happened with Hayk it would destroy me.

'That's why she hates me. She thinks Toke deserved better than me.' Paltino thumbs the crease in his pant leg, trying to avoid answering. I guess it wasn't really a question anyway. 'Well, I don't disagree with her.' I rock back against the cool bark and feel a little lighter knowing someone else loves Toke too. We take a moment in the red silence, sucking in the woody air through our noses, tingling in the chilly breeze to—I don't know—just breathe without thinking. It feels good.

'Is this always like this nowadays?' I press my thumb between Paltino's forever scrunched-up brow and gently pull it up to his hairline. He releases the wrinkle and his face relaxes, exposing that dimple faintly. 'Doesn't that feel better?' Proud of myself, I snuggle back into the earthy arms as if they were Axalte's. But they are not Axalte's. He's gone. I have lost him like I have lost so many. Except Paltino. Dimply, whiny, protective, heroic Paltino. I tilt my head and let the smooth desert breeze blow my hair in and out of my face. I drink him in. Is this that other life? The other life where 'we would be great together'? He twirls a lock of my hair on his finger and lets it spin out.

'Get some sleep, Suni.' We both lean on our sides, face each other on our respective branches and watch each other's eyelids get heavier with each lingering blink. Even in this rooted tree, knowing the truth of who I am, with my friend, under the moonlight, and with my body heavy with exhaustion I cannot sleep. What a ridiculous irony. So tired but unable to sleep? Do other such conditions exist? Do people ever get so hungry that they cannot eat? Or so rested that they cannot wake? Or so thirsty that they cannot drink? With everything that I have learned, why have I still not found the peace I need to sleep? What is left for me to know?

Paltino's eyes widen and he sits up, fixated on something over my shoulder. I whip my head around. Vehicles. Several. They are a good distance away.

'They can't be coming to us.' Paltino's brow is scrunched again, understandably.

'How can you be sure?'

'No one knows of this spot. This was where I was supposed to meet Fellie with Flora. This was Fellie's spot. No one knows about this but her and me. And she wouldn't have told them.'

'She would have never told them anything.'

'Why don't you just hear their thoughts and make sure?'

'It doesn't work that way. We can't just connect to anyone.'

'Then who can you connect to?'

'I can't tell you, yet. But don't worry. They can't be coming to us.'

The vehicles stay steady on their course. Far enough that all we see are the multiple lights on each one, on top, on the doors, in the front, on the sides—some brighter, some moving, but all pink out in the moonlight. They are headed in our direction but slightly west. They look as if they will pass us.

'Did you write down any of that stuff I read on memory acquisition?' Paltino pulls out his paper and sticks his nose in it. Not easy to read in red light. His eyes dart.

'You didn't open that tab. You just read the name "memory acquisition test results" and that's when the system discovered you.'

'What if they pulled that off, too? What if, just like they can extract a Mark's power, they can extract a Mark's memory?' I dig my thumbnail into the bark as we both watch the vehicles continue on their path just west of us. Now closer, we can make out their oversized tyres struggling through the deep sand and the cluster of heads bobbing inside.

'That's how they found Una and the other havens. That's how they discovered our identities.' The vehicles bank a hard turn. Dead on. 'They took Fellie's memories somehow and they know we are here.'

They are coming for us.

# Chapter 24

'They will come for you!' A woman's voice. Shaky, weak, but familiar.

We are in a cave. Una. A smaller, emptier Una: before the Risers, before the families, before the raid. Axalte and Paltino heave the woman by her bound feet. I bend down to her face and adjust the gag that has slipped out of her mouth and reposition her glasses. It's Ms Gord. Her sweater-cape trails behind her on the cave floor, barely hanging on to her chin as she struggles to hold her head up.

She kicks and screams periodically until her body tires and then she just cries and tries to talk to us through the gag.

'We can't understand you, Ms Gord, just try to relax.' Teen Me is genuinely irritated with her. I can feel it crawl up my skin—the disgust for others that an inflated sense of purpose brings. What have we done? Is this who I was?

Paltino pulls Ms Gord up and props her in a battered stolen Academy chair, the only piece of furniture in the cave. Teen Me places and lights candles in the crevices of the wall. Ms Gord coughs violently. The gag, wet with spit, pulls her lips taut across her large teeth. Her glasses are now somewhere between her forehead and head and her cape is long gone.

'I'm taking off her gag,' Axalte declares, his arms crossed and eyebrows bouncing as he glares at us, ready for a protest that never comes. He unties the gag, careful not to pull at her hair frizzy with dust from the ground.

'Mr Neem. Axalte, please. You're not like them; you're not an animal. Please help me.' Teen Me rolls her eyes with an exaggerated grunt and shoves the gag back in Ms Gord's mouth.

'We don't need to hear this.' Teen Me's level of comfort discomforts me. 'The tunnels are not stable and we haven't reinforced the walls in this space. Too much sound vibration can collapse them. So we can't just let her scream. And besides, it's annoying.'

'This is not right. Look at her. She's scared. We are supposed to be helping people, not torturing them.' Axalte grabs his head, sending his spikes boing-ing.

'She's been washed. You think she's going to welcome a reclaim? No one is. This is how every reclaim is going to be. They are going to cry. They are going to beg. They are going to be scared to death. But it's because they don't know better. They don't know we are saving them.' If only Teen Me knew that one day I would need 'saving'. Held down with elbows and knees in my stomach, on my arms. Hard hands squeezing my skull into place. Thick fingers muffling my mouth. That was my salvation.

'We are taking away her choice. The very thing we are trying to give them,' Axalte says.

'We have to take it back to give it to them. This is the only way. Right now they live an illusion. Any choices they make aren't real because they aren't fully informed. After the reclaim they can see, only then can they have a choice, a real choice.'

'But that's not why we have her here.' Paltino chews his lip. He's right. We just don't want to talk about it. 'We don't want to test the Reclaimer on Lute. We need a trial run. A lab rat. Let's not pretend we are saving anyone here, we are just experimenting. Just like the Experts during the Sterilization.'

We are nothing like the Experts. Nothing. Repeat it enough times until it becomes true. We are nothing like the Experts.

'It's going to work.' Teen Me is sure of it.

'You don't know that for sure.' Paltino doesn't take his eyes off Ms Gord. He can't even look at me right now. That's not a good sign.

'I know it enough that I was willing to do it to you, Paltino.'

'But that was before you discovered the anomalies. Now, you know there is a chance this could fry her.'

'Better her than Lute,' I say. Paltino agrees, I know he does even though he doesn't want to say it.

'Why? Why is his life more valuable than hers?' Axalte steps backwards as he speaks as if he's shrinking.

'We've been through this. We all knew that there was a risk with the first reclaim and we all agreed that we didn't want to risk Lute's life. We all agreed on that. It's a simple choice—Ms Gord's life or Lute's.' I try to calm Axalte, try to bring him back in.

'It's not right, Suni.' Axalte has shrunk into the shadows.

'Isn't that why we came this far? Because we all know that this is the only way. You have to trust me. I know this will work.' Ms Gord yelps as she twists and squirms her round body, unable to move but unable to stop trying. Poor little chipfin.

'I can't do this. We can't do this.' Axalte is pleading now.

'This is freedom. Messy. Risky. You want everything to be perfect? Get washed.' I pull out the Reclaimer and press it against Ms Gord's skull. She shakes her head back and forth. I can't position it correctly.

'Hold her head.' Axalte recoils further. 'It's okay, Axalte.' Paltino looks at me, brow scrunched but he's looking at me. That's a good sign. 'Hold her head, Paltino. I promise you she will be fine. I promise you.' Paltino grabs Ms Gord's head tight. She wildly blinks out streams of tears and her chest heaves with phlegmy sobs. I press the Reclaimer on to her weathered brow and a bright light shines into her skull. Her body falls limp and her eyelids drop.

Paltino and I release her. Axalte shudders in his shadowy corner. I think he's crying. She's not moving. We wait for what feels like hours. The candles' flames burn still and straight up as if they were paintings. I think we are all holding our breath.

We are nothing like the Experts. This was the only way. We are nothing like the Experts.

All Seggies were rounded up like cattle and herded into cages. Back then they weren't called Seggies—they were just from 'underprivileged countries' in the East. The Experts—no,

*Doctors—were from 'developed countries' in the West, the first who couldn't have babies. When a year had gone by since anyone from the West had become pregnant they became desperate. They poked, prodded and eventually cut up the people from the East trying to find out why they could still get pregnant when they themselves could not. But they couldn't understand. There were theories, lots of theories. Pharmaceuticals, genetically modified foods, plastics in the ocean, uranium deposits in the earth, alien body snatchers, estrogen in the water, God punishing the wicked. Just theories.*

*Eventually, the Experts figured that their races would die out if they didn't start forced reproduction with those who still could birth. Every race, religion and nation afraid to be bred out competed in the perverse biological baby race. They believed they were doing the right thing for the preservation of their humanity. It was not out of a will to subjugate, oppress or dehumanize but out of a desire to save themselves. But it did subjugate, oppress and dehumanize and if you take everything away from someone, even their dignity, all that remains is a dangerous monster with nothing to lose. And so came The Cleanse and then there was only death. And all that mattered was the death.*

*We are nothing like the Experts.*

*Ms Gord rustles and turns. We hurry over to her and rip off her gag and ropes. Her face turns to mine and she places a hand on my cheek.*

*'My baby. I had a baby.' Tears streak out of her wide-open eyes. She does not blink them away; she does not hide them. She*

*had a memory. It worked. Paltino grabs me in a tight hug. Over his shoulder I see Axalte staring down at Ms Gord. 'They took my baby.' Ms Gord buckles in a deep sob. The sob that her truth brings. It's infectious and I have to look away and cover my ears. But I can still hear her through my hands. I hate the sound of these cries. This does not feel like salvation. But it is. Teen Me reminds herself. It is salvation. It is salvation.*

*'Did you know?' Axalte's eyes on Ms Gord. He steps into the candlelight that trembles from Ms Gord's sobs. His massive width shrivels with the roll of his shoulders forward as his back hunches into a round mound. He's still wilting. 'Did you know for sure or did you gamble?' He turns his wet eyes to mine.*

*He's never lost anyone. He has never suffered as Paltino and I have. Suffering rips you down to your root. So what grows back is stronger, more grounded, deeper, more determined. Suffering lets you make choices that you couldn't have made before because now you know the cost if you don't and you will do anything to prevent that from happening to you ever again. My oak of a man, with his wide-open chest and thick limbs, my giant who sends shivers into officers' knees until they clunk against each other like defective robots, my huge love with his inescapable grip— inescapable for even me—my strong man is not strong enough.*

*'I knew.' He squeezes my hand and pulls me into his thick, woody, huge embrace. He bends his neck and buries his nose in my hair as if to inhale me.*

*'I want to believe that, Suni. I have to believe that.' This is a different kind of strength. This is my kind of strength.*

# Chapter 25

Paltino grabs my hand and pulls me down the tree. My knee slams against a protruding root and the rest of me collapses into its knots and bulges. I don't bother to untangle myself from its clutches.

I'm hungry. I'm tired. I'm hurt and I'm broken. Everyone is dead or gone. I don't want to run anymore. There is no point. The vehicles are so close now that I have to squint in their pink lights. Just come and take me. I'm done.

'Ami sacrificed herself to protect you. It was her purpose. If you let them take you then you are robbing her of her purpose. Then her death, Fellie's, the Havens, Buzz . . . it would all be pointless.' Paltino stretches out his hand to mine, giving me the choice. Do I live or do I die? Do I fight or do I rest? Who am I? What do I want? What is this all for? Why have they all sacrificed themselves for me? What do they think I can do? What do they see in me that I cannot?

Paltino blurs to a shadow. His face comes in and out of focus as the world spins around me. My heavy head teeters on my neck. First, I feel his stale breath in a giant gust on my forehead and cheeks. It smells like earth. Not the desert sand or the rocky cave but earth, from the Old World, damp and cool. It's Hayk. He leans close to me and whispers, *'It's time to run, Suni.'* And just like that he's gone.

*'It's time to run, Suni.'* I grip Paltino's hand and yank my limbs out of the roots' knotted hold. The vehicles rip into a sandblazing stop. The doors fly open and Hunters burst out from the doors, the top and the back. Paltino steers me into the tunnel but not before I count them. One. Two. Three. Four—that's Joyli. Five. The entire Legion. *Run harder, Suni.*

Remember these tunnels. I know these tunnels. I know every low hanging rock, every sunken space and every ridge in the uneven floor. *Run, Suni. Run.* Boots stomp behind us. They have followed us into the cave. We have to lose them in another tunnel. Then I remember we can't lose them. If they took the Mark's memories then they know this cave just as well as we do. We are not going to be able to escape them.

Paltino turns, pushes me aside and storms towards them.

'Run, Suni. I will hold them off.' And then the black tunnel devours him. No. Not Paltino. This is not his purpose. I won't let it be. I refuse. I will not leave him here. I will not lose him. I grab his arm and bring him back to me.

'*The tunnels are not stable. Too much sound vibration can collapse them.*' Smart, sexy, spunky, cheeky, fearless Teen Me. I plug my ears with my fingers and scream. The kind of scream that forces my eyelids shut, the kind of scream that squeezes my gut and pulls my chest down to my knees. Suck in and inflate my lungs until my chest balloons. Repeat.

Paltino follows suit. I can't see or hear him but I can feel the vibrations of his deep scream on my skin. Repeat.

Pebbles jump around my foot and the walls quake. A hot blast of air blows the hair from my face and dirt into my mouth. It worked. Boulders fall from the tunnel ceiling like giant raindrops smashing on the ground, splashing everywhere—into my ankles, shins, stomach.

*Run, Suni. Run harder.* Did we lose them? The tunnel forks, we veer left. The vibration of the last collapsing tunnel reverberates to this one. It shakes violently, forcing our run into a staggered walk as we hold on to the crumbling walls. A jagged rock slices through Paltino's right arm. If he yelped I couldn't hear him. Red moonlight seeps in from a crevice ahead. The exit is gone. We are in a dead end. Behind us boots shuffle on the wobbly ground. We are trapped in the suffocating dirt-dry, thick air.

'Suni, do you want to swim?' Hayk's voice tiptoes in my head.

I know this tunnel, this is my tunnel, this is Hayk's tunnel. I press my ear against the rumbling wall and can hear the splashing water. I can do this. We can do this. Thank you, Hayk.

Paltino. Come to me. I feel along the wall. He follows. I know it's here somewhere. I know it is. I scuff backwards towards the thumping boots. My hands find a round rock bulging from the wall like a pregnant belly. The rock belly. 'We can go inside and slide it back to close us in like secrets.' You knew, Hayk. You knew all along.

We roll the rock belly out to the side and crawl into the space. The smell of the cool pool water quenches my dirt-dry nostrils. The sparkly blue water splashes and spills like a glass of water in a shaky hand and its twinkly reflections dance along the cave wall.

We slowly pull the rock belly back to close us off. My hands, wet with sweat, slip on the sharp edges but I keep pulling. Just a few inches left . . . when a large hand grabs the rock belly from the other side. It's one of them. They've found us.

No time. Paltino and I turn and dive into the sploshing pool. The current throws us in different directions. I smash against the floor and what little air was left in me escapes in tiny bubbles. Through the white frothy water I see a narrow underwater tunnel. Our exit. It hasn't collapsed.

A body dives into the pool just a few feet behind me. It's a Hunter. The water thrashes us against each other. I push off his chest and swim towards the tunnel. He takes my foot and jerks me back. I stomp my foot into his face and propel off. The thrust launches me into the tunnel's current.

Pulled, pushed, spinning, tumbling, I plummet through the underwater tunnel tube until it tosses me out on to a bank in a large cave opening. I roll on my knees and vomit water until I can breathe. Moonlight peeks in from the cracks and tiny holes in thin shards of red. My hands, knees, ribs sting and throb. Blood pools beneath me. I don't even know where I am bleeding from and all I can think about is Paltino. Where is Paltino?

I watch the spout of the tunnel tube and feel my bottom lip crumple into a quiver. Paltino. Please. I can't do this alone. Paltino, I need you. Please. I love you, Paltino. This is our other life. This is it. Please, Paltino. I bang my now numb fists against my thighs. Please.

The tunnel tosses a body on to the bank. Paltino? No, it's the Hunter, mangled and still. His large body covers most of the bank. He's the tall man. The Commander. His thick and long arms lie contorted around him. I would stand no chance against this man with or without a dose. I watch his back for a moment. It gently rises and falls. He is breathing. I grab a nearby rock and run over to him. I have to get him before he wakes up.

I turn him over and raise the rock over my head to slam it down on his face. My eyes, the moon, the water, the air, the world . . . everything freezes on his face.

It's Axalte.

# Chapter 26

'Axalte!' Teen Me stares down at the giant man spread out over the sandy dune, tongue hanging out, eyes crossed, arms limp. Teen Me rolls her eyes, clearly unimpressed. 'We don't have time for this. Get up.' I rock him gently with my foot. Nothing.

Paltino creeps up behind me, eyebrows knitted. 'Maybe you flipped him too hard. I did tell you that was going to happen, eventually.' No way. Not buying it.

I slip the gun off my shoulder and pounce on him, sticking my twitchy fingers in the inside of his elbow, the squishy part on his side between his ribs and his hips, right behind his ear where his hairline meets his neck—all his uncontrollable spots. He buckles and whips his giant body around as he bellies a rumbling laugh. I smash his head into the sand.

'You're wasting time.'

He grabs my hand. 'Maybe sometimes we should.' He pulls me down into him and presses his lips against mine. He buries his nose in the black thickness of my hair and inhales me. I lose myself in it. In the sandy, inappropriate, irresponsible, messiness *of it—of him—almost to the point where I don't notice Paltino pulling his eyes away. Almost.*

*I pluck myself off Axalte, feigning irritation, but I can't wipe the dreamy glaze from my eyes. I can see him drink in my gooeyness. I sling the gun back on my shoulder and open my mouth to shout some cheeky nonsense when Paltino pulls me down into the sand. Axalte, elbows in the sand, crawls over.*

*We peek over the edge of the dune to the rows of the Pangean homes. These are the single family models. Same wide door, same windowed foyer, same sloping roof. Same coloured poppyflies (this month it's all about blue), same stoned walkway, same fake grass, same sun-warped plastic mailboxes.*

*Teen Me may be used to these but I want to go back to the poppyflies. The same ones from the field with Axalte—the first memory I had. Round poofy balls of colour with long-stem legs and tiny dangly feet. Flowers that can't help but fly even knowing that in doing so they will die. They fly almost as soon as they bloom so their lifespans are only minutes. Pretty little suicidal decorations. The Pangeans pick them up and stand them on their thin legs, decorating yards and dinner tables with their lifeless carcasses. This month it's all about blue.*

*'Which one?' Paltino whispers to me.*

*'2387. It should be the third one in the fifth row.'*

*'What? Are we just going to walk over and ring the bell?' Axalte shakes the sand out of his spikes as he speaks.*

*'Basically.' Paltino and I nod.*

'Oh, okay.' Axalte sticks his thick finger in his ear and even though it doesn't fit, he twists trying to scoop out some sand. I giggle at his absurdity. Teen Me giggled a lot. 'Well, can we get up then?'

We all rise. Three officers strapped with guns. Three Risers hiding in plain sight. We stroll down the dune and blend into the Pangean street. Don't walk too fast or too slow. Don't look too sad or too happy. Don't be too quiet or too loud. Everything in moderate, controlled little doses. Sometimes maybe we should just waste a little time.

Paltino's dimple is as flat as this road. I can see his itchy thoughts scraping away at the inside of his forehead. He wears his worry on his face. No, he advertises his worry on his face. Or maybe I just know him too well. He reaches for his crescent necklace and flicks it between his thumb and index finger. He's listening to me right now, isn't he? Bouncey bubblebutts bludgeon bumbling boobies.

His dimple deepens as he unknits his brow. He looks at me out of the corner of his eye as he feigns coolness.

'What exactly is a bubblebutt?'

We both smile at our inside joke, leaving Axalte a little confused. Paltino doesn't explain it to him. Neither do I. But he doesn't mind. And then we arrive.

Axalte and I fall back. Paltino should do this. This is Lute's house. We are here to take him. I wish I could warn Teen Me and tell her what this will do to Lute. But I am helpless here as I suppose everyone is when recalling their memories. When *you remember something, you have already lived it so you have already felt it. But this is not the same thing. I am reliving these moments as if they are happening right now, feeling them for the first time, the pain, the love, the fear, the happiness, without any control and without playing any part in them—in total resignation. Not really my thing.*

*Paltino presses his shaky finger on the doorbell. We hang our heads, exhale, inhale, tap our feet, look around. Nothing. He rings again.*

*'Good day,' a man's voice calls from the neighbouring house. He plods up to his doorstep and flips his hand in the air in a listless greeting. Pangeans always greet their neighbours.*

*'Good . . .' I cannot even complete the phrase as I focus on this man. I know this man. He's the officer from the cave. The one who had a sick wife. The one who shot his commanding officer. The one who tore me from my mother in the back of the car. The one who gave me to Bearlett and Lina. This is the officer who took my mother.*

*Every cell in my body wants to throw myself off this porch, fling myself on him, lash my limbs around him, sink my teeth into him and carry him to some place dark, some place quiet, some place far . . .*

*Paltino places his hand on my shoulder and calms me. I have to wait. We are here for Lute. Let's get him first. The door opens and Lute stands there. His eyes wash over Paltino and flicker between us all. Paltino's jaw hangs open and he doesn't bother blinking the gathering tears in his eyes.*

*'Lute?' Paltino's voice cracks under the weight of it all.*

'Yes. Can I help you?' Lute wipes a plate dry and tosses the damp towel over his shoulder—it gives off the 'I do this all the time' feeling but we know he really doesn't. I mean not the real him. His face is relaxed, not too happy, not too sad. He is a pleasant, polite, stiff robot. He gestures for us to enter but we don't. Paltino just stares at him, his brother who he has, who we have sought, for almost a year. And here he is, right here. Finally. And he has no idea who we are. We all knew he was washed and we all knew he wouldn't remember us or even himself, for that matter. But it's one thing to know something and another to see something. His indifference, even though involuntary, is painful and cruel.

My eyes go back to the officer. He slogs his way into his house. He's older and fatter now. His cold hands felt like heavy lead cuffed on my twig arms as he ripped me from my mother. I was just a child, a scrawny little cave monster. Not now. Now I could rip him apart with my bare hands. This monster is all grown up.

Axalte nudges us to enter the house. We do. There isn't much to notice about the house. As pleasant, polite and bland as fake Lute. I immediately go to the window on the left and search for the officer in the neighbouring house. I see his head bob here and there. His figure passes from one window to another. He bumps into a table and scurries to clean up after himself. He's moving quickly, no, he's rushing from room to room upstairs, downstairs, opening drawers and closets, fumbling along the way. He's looking for something.

'Where's your wife?' Axalte asks Lute.

'She's in the fields. She should be home in about an hour.'

'Okay, we can wait.' Axalte dives into the sofa. The mushy, squishy Pangean sofas. Paltino is unable to say or do much, crippled by Lute's indifference. I don't take my eyes off the officer and his peculiarity.

'Sir, can you come here for a moment?' I wave Lute over casually and then switch to an official demand for compliance. Lute's canvas flip-flops pitter-patter over. Transmit, receive, process. 'You see that man in that house next door?' Lute presses his nose up to the window as he desperately peers about as if this is some test and a failure on this test would result in some horrific punishment. I put my hand on his shoulder. This sends him staggering back. 'It's okay, Lute. No one is going to hurt you. Just tell me if you know that man.' Lute creeps to the window again. So much of what is going on here is unPangean but our uniforms won't let him question us. He's programmed not to ever question us.

'No.'

'Are you saying he's not your neighbour?'

'No, is that what this is all about?' Lute struggles to maintain the smile on his face.

I watch the officer throw books off the shelves, hurl plates out of the cupboards and yank out drawers and their contents. He stops in the middle of the room and catches his breath. He's giving up. He's going to leave.

'Paltino. We don't have time. We'll come back for his wife.' I don't take my eyes off the officer.

'What? What's happening? What do you want with my wife?' Lute's buffoony voice is such an insult to the secure determination his real voice carries.

'Suni, we can't do that. They will redistribute her and we'll lose her.' Paltino is pleading. What difference does it make? She was washed to love Lute anyway. They are strangers to each other. When we reclaim him he won't even think about her. Every thought, every memory, every moment was fake between them. And I wasn't really asking you, Paltino. I was telling you.

But Teen Me is wrong. I was washed but what I felt for Toke was real. I may not have loved him like I loved Axalte but what I felt for him was real because it survived the reclaim. In fact, what I felt for him strengthened after the reclaim because it was only after that that I was able to see who he really was and what he was willing to compromise for me.

'What is it?' Axalte, out of the mind-reading loop, comes to the window and watches the officer tear at his hair and smash random figurines against the walls—more animals in clothes, puppies in scarves, piglets in bonnets. 'Who is it?'

'The way to my mother.' Axalte traces a line from my eyebrow to my chin and his eyes smile at me. That's his way of saying he's 'with me' but I knew that all along. We both look back at the officer. He stares straight at us, teeth exposed, hands fisted, knuckles white, knees bent. I can see his lips twitch from his growl. He's going to run. This is no Pangean officer—or maybe that's what he's thinking of us.

'Suni, please don't. We have to get Lute out safely.' Paltino is still pleading. I don't blame him. He is fighting for his family and I am fighting for mine and he has always been overcautious. Also not my thing. Paltino, I cannot lose him. 'This is the only hope of finding my mother I have had in the last ten years. Axalte and you can get Lute out. I will meet you in Una.'

'Suni! Please!' Paltino lunges for my arm and Axalte holds him back.

The officer zooms out of the house, sending papers and knick-knacks flying. I throw my body over the sofa and hurtle out of the front door, leaving Axalte to control Paltino and both of them to secure Lute. We have exposed ourselves. They have just minutes to get him out of there. They can do it. I see the rabid officer pushing through a lazy crowd of robots and zombies oohing and aahing at the newest bluest poppyfly carcasses.

He catches a glimpse of me barrelling down the flat street towards him and he stumbles into a nearby house. I see him fumble through the house and I turn left, running alongside the house so when he barges out of the back, I'm just a few feet behind him.

He tries to lift his tired clunky feet faster. He pushes forward with his swinging fists but his breathing is short and loud and I know he has moments until he's in my grasp.

I widen my strides to gain momentum. I'm just a step behind. I leap forward and land my left foot on to his left calf and push myself up to perch on his shoulders. I slide my legs over his shoulders and under his armpits, locking my feet at the ankles at his shoulder blades, pushing his back into an extreme arch.

*I slip my right arm under his chin and back up to his ear. I grab my right elbow just under his chin and with the full force of my arms apply deep pressure to his neck—cutting out his oxygen. He clunks around for a few steps and then collapses into the sand. His eyes roll back to white, strings of saliva fling from his mouth and his face blues. I let go of his neck before he dies but hold on to it a second or two or three longer than I need to.*

*This month is all about the blue.*

# Chapter 27

Muddy water from the rock suspended in the air above me trickles down my face and stings my eyes. This is the only affirmation that this is real. I can feel the sting. This must be real. This is not a dream. This is not a memory. This is Axalte.

I can't hear the water spewing on the rocky bank or see the shards of moonlight guiding the way out. I don't realize that the Hunters must be on their way or remember that Paltino still has not emerged from that tunnel. All I know now is Axalte. My Axalte.

He's bigger than I remember him—each arm round and stiff like he's stuffed them with rocks. His brow, jaw and cheekbones are sharper now, casting darker shadows and deepening the hollows under his eyes and in his cheeks; he looks almost skeletal—vicious, severe, empty. His skin hangs on his face, worn and heavy. He looks much older than he should. Pain, no matter how hidden and how buried, ages us. I finally put the rock down and slide over to him. I run my fingers through his springy spiked hair and watch the coils boing back into place.

'What have they done to you?' I trace a line from his eyebrow to his chin. This time it's my way of saying I am with him. The real me with the real him. He gurgles; his chest, wide and square labours to rise and fall before stilling. He's not breathing.

I weave my fingers, one hand over the other, lock my elbows out, raise myself on my knees and push the heel of my hand into his breastbone—deep and release. Repeat. Again. Breathe, Axalte. Again. Quick. Quicker. My wet hair lashes my face. Again. My hands squeezed white . . . tight. Again.

I tilt his forehead back and his chin up, dropping open his mouth. I pinch his nose and cover his mouth with mine. I push in a quick forceful breath and watch his chest rise. Again. He's still not breathing.

Heel of my hand on his breastbone. Push. Push. Quick. Again. I am not going to let this happen. I don't get him back just to lose him. Quick. Again. No. I won't let this happen. I won't lose him. Quick.

I wrap my mouth around his and blow in two breaths and go back to pumping. At some point the tunnel tube spews Paltino out and he crawls over to me, confused. I don't fully realize that he's there and I don't stop.

I wrap my mouth around Axalte's and blow again. Back to pumping. Paltino just sits there for a few minutes or a few hours, puking water every now and then—time is weird right now; it feels long and short at the same time. When he's done he tries to stop me.

I must be covered in sweat now because whatever is dribbling into my mouth is salty. Sweat or blood. Or maybe I just threw up too. My arms are tired and begin to feel like noodles. I have to clench my teeth to draw the energy to keep my elbows straight and I have to keep shaking the dizziness from my head. There's not enough air in here. I don't care. I won't lose Axalte.

'Suni, we don't have a Reclaimer. He's been washed. You can't wake him right now. We won't be able to stop him if you save him. Not with his powers. He's not Axalte. He's a Hunter.' Paltino tries to pull me off Axalte. The more he tugs at me the more I jerk myself back to Axalte. I curse him for making me waste what little energy I have left on fighting him off me.

'What do you want me to do? Just let him die?'

'He would have wanted me to protect you.'

'That's the problem with you, Paltino. You never understood that I don't need you to protect me.' I throw myself back on Axalte and pump his chest. Two forceful blows into his mouth. Pumping.

Paltino throws himself on top of me, his chest against my back, slings one arm around my neck and flips on to his back, snatching me off Axalte and on to him—all in one fluid motion. I don't have enough left in me to stop him.

My back to his chest, he winds his legs around me from underneath, pinning my legs down and raises a syringe to my neck. I can't move. His arm around my neck tightens. I kick and squirm but he's got me and I can't even scream.

'I'm so sorry, Suni. But I have to save you.'

I pull my elbow into my body and feel under me for Paltino's stomach. There it is. I lift my arm up and with the full force of my body jam my elbow into his stomach. Again. And again until I hear the hit blow out his air and he drops the syringe and me.

I flip over and punch him square in the jaw. He crumples over, desperate to suck in air as I crawl back on to Axalte and resume pumping and blowing air into his lungs until I feel his lips move under mine. I pull up and tilt his head to the side as he coughs out water that looks like blood in the moonlight. His coughs get deeper and roll into full-body heaves as water sprays everywhere. I rub his back as he continues to retch. His eyes are opening now. I bend down, press my cheek to his and kiss his temple.

My lips on his skin sends jitters through me, like Buzz's little electric shocks—a little painful, a little tingly, but completely unlike anything else. My tummy flips and turns in tickly knots, pulling me into him and I can't help but want to giggle. This is what love feels like—giggly, tickly, involuntary, electric nausea.

I have to pull my lips from him but I want to see his eyes. It's been so long since I have lost myself in them.

Now that he's fully awake I can see what this time has done to him. His brow is heavy, his cheeks are sucked in and his lips are thinned. He is just a shadow of who he was, but a shadow I can hold and feel. This shadow is enough for me.

His deep almond eyes—shiny and twinkly—focus on to mine and I feel weight fall from my back until I am a light and airy Teen Me again. I never lost him; even when I was washed he came to me every night and slipped his arm around me—he was there when I had no one. The wash could not wash him from me and I knew that the wash could not wash me from him. I knew we did not need a Reclaimer for him. The love we have is different. No technology can erase it, just like no technology can create it. I don't even want to consider what Paltino almost did here. I don't want to think about what I almost lost because of him or what he almost did to me. I just want to breathe this all in—I just want to breathe . . . Axalte's eyes narrow and his lips press into a line. I see that first before I feel his thumbs pressing into my throat. My face floods with hot blood that slams against the back of my eyeballs. He sits up, holding me by the neck like a doll and rolls over me—I'm on the ground and he's squeezing my neck as he perches on top of me.

He grinds his teeth and pulses the muscles in his jaw. He looks like he's enjoying this. I don't even care that I'm about to die. I just can't believe that Axalte will be the one who kills me. He will never forgive himself. Him killing me would destroy us both. I suppose it all makes sense. We would become another one of Pangea's ridiculous ironies: lovers who destroy what they love.

Paltino springs up behind Axalte and plunges the same syringe in Axalte's neck. Axalte's eyelids immediately drop and he collapses on top of me. His expansive chest smothers me as both Paltino and I struggle to flip his heavy body off me.

I bend at the waist and use every muscle to pull in as much air as possible. I see Paltino wince as he moves. Did I break his rib?

'No, you didn't. I should have known better. You'd have never left him. That should knock him out for twelve hours. I mean that's what it would do to a regular person. I don't know what these doses he's been taking has done to his metabolism. By the size of him I'm guessing we've got maybe half that to get him somewhere and reclaim him. I just don't know where. Anywhere I would have taken him they already know about. All the Riser spots aren't safe.'

'Joyli's house. It's empty and she's been washed so she won't even remember it.'

'Okay, Malti will meet us there.' Oh right, all Marks can connect with each other. I had forgotten that part and started to think Paltino and I shared a special secret connection. But I remember now.

'Where is she?'

'She's still with Toke. He's fine.'

The journey to Joyli's house is chopped up and fuzzy, as if I'm remembering it and not really experiencing it. I think I may be slipping in and out of consciousness. I remember Paltino and me—veins bulging—struggling to haul Axalte out of the cave. Somewhere I slipped and skinned my elbow. There's always a weird sting from a superficial wound. It hurts but it's more annoying than painful so the sting is more mental than physical.

Then somehow we are in one of the Hunters' cars. I try to prop up Axalte's slumped body and Paltino fidgets with the dozens of knobs and dials. By the time he figures out how to drive it, I remove the tracker and snap it on to a tumbletree. That should keep them busy for a while. That's pretty funny. I burst out into a roaring laugh at the thought of all these bloodthirsty doped-up Hunters with their gadgets, guns and wound-up faces hot on the trail of the fleeing criminal mastermind: the tumbletree!

I wake up to my head whacking against the car's window. We are in a Pangean city: East. I don't know if I fell asleep, rested my head on the window and a bump slammed my head or if my head just crashed into the window as I fell asleep. I'm not sure what difference it makes but in one scenario I may have got to sleep for a few moments, which makes me feel better. I think I'll stick with that version. But one thing is for sure—Paltino's driving is worse than Toke's. Somewhere along the way

I must have explained how to get to Joyli's house because here we are. Rows and rows of townhouses. Pangea's newest harvest, ripe for the plucking.

The red moonlight is quickly retracting as the rising sun pours over the sandy horizon in its sleepy morning blues. A wave of blue chasing a wave of red. The Cleanse left layers of radiation and pollution in the sky so the sun now wakes in phases. It rises in hues of sleepy blues; the rays feel cool and warm at the same time like hot mint. This is when the sun is the safest, when it's not fully here yet. But this only lasts for minutes and as the sun wakes in its full angry, blinding yellow rage, it blasts through Pangea with all its carnivorous fury. I glance at Axalte.

My mind still choppy, I find myself breaking a window and unlocking the back door. The house is the same mess that Toke and I left it in. The shattered ballerina is on the floor. Somehow we must have got Axalte in the house—there he is, tied up and sleeping. His face blurs in and out.

'It's dehydration.' Paltino pulls me to the kitchen and we take turns sticking our whole heads under the faucet, letting the water fill our mouths and pour into our eyes. We chuckle and wipe our faces with our sleeves like naughty little kids. I can hear the water in my otherwise empty belly swoosh around. We take an inventory of the food options: stale bread, uncooked lentils, an entire sour pie and one roasted chicken leg.

Before we can ration it and save some for later it's all gone and all that's left is Paltino and me licking our lips and fingers and stretching with the satisfaction that a full belly brings. Naughty little cave monsters.

I wash my hands and run my wet fingers along my wild, loose hair, shaking out dirt, sand and other remnants of the last few hours. I twist it up and let it rest on my shoulder like a black tornado. I didn't realize Paltino was watching me. He quickly lowers his gaze and plucks at his chin bristles.

I don't know what to say to him. I don't even know what to think. I just try not to think about it. I don't want him to hear anything that will hurt him anymore than I already have.

With a blank mind I inspect the damage I did to his stomach. Deep purple bruises spread across his midriff like continents. Internal bleeding. No broken bones.

He notices my elbow and pulls me to the sink. Brow clenched, he pours water on my elbow from his cupped hand until it runs dry and then pats it clean with his fingers. He's concentrating so hard, it's kinda funny. Paltino, always dressing my wounds.

'About what I said in the cave.' He doesn't take his eyes off the raw fleshy patch. 'It's not true, you know. I do need you. I do need you to protect me.' He fills his hand with more water and continues to pour it on my elbow.

'Don't do that. Don't say things because you think I need to hear them.' He blows my wound dry, pulls off some leaves from a half-dead plant and proceeds to wrap my elbow. 'No helder leaves but these should protect the open wound from infection.' He releases my arm and washes his hands. He continues without looking at me. That's how I know I did something that hurt him . . . when he can't bring himself to look at me. 'We should check on Axalte.'

I mosey behind him like a scolded child, knowing I did something really bad but not exactly sure what I did. I keep my eyes on his heels and dig my nail into my thumb's cuticle until I can feel a small chunk of skin. I grab it and peel it away, ignoring the tingly sting. We both stare down at the sleeping Axalte. Paltino reinforces the restraints with whatever he can find—tape, rope, electrical cords. I don't bother. I know he won't hurt me.

'Malti will get here soon. One hour, maybe two, tops. She'll get here before he wakes.' It sounds like he's trying to reassure himself. He fluffs up the sofa pillows and pulls me down. 'Try to sleep, Suni. You need to.'

I don't sleep. I slip into the mushy sofa and curl up into a pillow. Paltino slides down on to the floor beside me and positions himself so he's directly between Axalte and me. Always trying to protect me.

My eyes don't move from Axalte. His long-lashed eyes flutter beneath his closed lids. I know he's in there. Just like the real Joyli was in her. I just have to get to him. I have to find the path to him. And with my eyes on his I feel my eyelids drop and for the first time in as long as I can remember without any thinking or dreaming or worrying . . . I sleep.

\* \* \*

It takes me a minute to remember who I am, where I am, why I am here and why I should not pummel Paltino for waking me.

I look up and see Axalte, still tied in his chair, motionless but now wide-eyed and fully awake. He's not struggling to get free; with his powers he should have been able to melt those makeshift restraints and kill us by now. But he's just sitting there, staring at us with his eyes narrow and intense. I remember each dose has a certain amount of hours that it lasts for. So, maybe his powers wore off and he hasn't broken free because he can't.

No, that's not it. My Axalte is in there still. I know it. That's why he's just sitting here, that's why he hasn't killed us yet. Something in him is stopping him. Something he doesn't understand, yet. But that something in him is pushing against his wash that made him the Commander of the Legion. We can't tell him who he really is. We have to reclaim him. And even then we will have to wait until he remembers who he is, as

Paltino has done for me, with much more patience than I think I have.

But right now we have to stall and buy time for Malti to arrive with the Reclaimer. He thinks he is the Commander of the Legion about to be interrogated by Riser scum, so let's play that game. Paltino throws me a wink of acknowledgement and I wipe out the sleep from my eyes and saunter over to a table and sit on it, swinging my legs in the most casually aggressive way I can.

'Do you know who we are?' I point to Paltino with my eyebrows and tilt my head up so I'm talking down to him and my eyes are but a sliver open. Like a Hunter.

'Maybe. Do you know who *I* am?' His voice. Warm honey.

'Yes. Axalte. The Commander of the Legion.' I swirl the sound of his name around my mouth like a sweet candy. I can feel love oozing from my pores. I don't even know how to hide it. I'm trying to look hard but I probably just look like a lush.

'So you are stupid, then.' Axalte's words are like a slap.

'Excuse me?'

'I am saying that you are stupid, stupid. Because only a stupid Riser would save the life of the Commander and then keep him as a souvenir. You know I can't say that stupidity is a common trait for you Riser scum. I mean from all the Risers we've caught and from all their minds that we drained before we killed them, not many of them were stupid per se. Mutants, yes. Dirty, yes. Smelly, yes. But not stupid. But then again you are both Seggies, Seggies are always stupid.'

Who is this monster? At least now I have stopped oozing love. Maybe I *am* stupid.

'Where are the Risers from the havens? Where have you taken them?' Paltino doesn't have a hard time sounding pissed off.

'What's the matter, Seggie? Do I need to speak slower? They are dead. We killed them. All of them.' That hits us like a sledgehammer in the gut.

This is not my Axalte.

'Suni, this isn't a good idea. We need to shut him up. We can't see him like this, we won't be able to forget it. And we can't let the others know. This isn't an easy thing to forgive.' Paltino is right.

Paltino rams his right hook into Axalte's jaw, sending his head whipping to the left. Axalte spits out some blood and blows Paltino a kiss.

'Is that all you got, sweetie? You plan on reclaiming me? Let me guess . . . you knew me before the wash. What? Were we like best friends? Siblings? What?' Each word is a knife in my chest that just keeps twisting and twisting. 'What about the girl? What were we? Lovers? That's it, isn't it? We were lovers. And you've been reclaimed so you love me and I don't even know who you are.' He breaks out in that deep belly laugh of his which I adored once.

I grab the only unbroken vase and smash it into the side of his head. He roars as he shakes it off. He's too strong. An officer's vehicle pulls up in front of the house. Malti? Malti has a car?

'That's not Malti.' Paltino backs away from the window.

'You see, we are not dirty Marks. So we can only use one power at a time.' The ropes around Axalte begin to smoke and sizzle. Within seconds they melt away. Flora's power. He can only use one power at a time?

All this time we thought we were stalling him but he was the one who was stalling. He was using the power to connect to the other Hunters and tell him where he was; that's why he couldn't melt away the restraints. He was just baiting us into a conversation until they arrived. I look out the window and see Joyli and the Hunters stampede to the door.

Paltino and I clasp hands. We can't survive this. Joyli blasts open the door and collapses into Axalte's arms like something out of the Old World movies minus the ringlets and the poofy dress. He drapes her on his side like a fashion accessory and arches his eyebrow at me.

'Sorry, honey. You're not my type.' Axalte gives a cocksure chuckle and bends down to Joyli. I squeeze my eyes tight before their lips meet. I can't see this.

# Chapter 28

'I can't wait to see this.' Teen Me paces in front of the tied-up officer she—me—I apprehended—the officer who took me from my mother. I puff my chest and breathe loudly through my flared nostrils as I circle my mounted trophy. Teen Me looks like a Hunter. He blubbers some gibberish and tries to eat through the gag. I dance around on my tiptoes, stretching my neck as if I'm prepping for a fight.

We are in Una. A more established Una sprinkled with homey things: tattered but comfy-looking sofas, a tray of contorted paint tubes, an uneven dining table with mismatched chairs, some cooking stuff, a few narrow beds covered in sheets with faded floral designs and towers of teetering books. Whatever we could swipe from unoccupied homes. When someone is pulled out of their homes and washed, they aren't given the time to pack. And so as they leave behind their half-lived lives they also leave behind a home full of half-used things. As we reclaim more people, some may just get reunited with their former chairs, bathrobes and curtains.

*Axalte and Paltino hustle in, gently carrying a passed-out Lute and place him on one of the beds. Paltino adjusts the pillow under his head.*

'What happened?' I interrogate.

'He wouldn't stop fighting us. I had no choice, I had to knock him out.' *Axalte scrunches up his face and scratches his head, sending his spikes boing-ing around. Paltino and I synchronize an* 'Oooooooooh.'

'He's gonna be so pissed at you.' *Paltino's face is relaxed for the first time in a year. Brow released and dimple in its full indented glory.*

'Yeah, I know. I'm looking forward to the lecture.' *We all just soak in that for a minute, like achy feet in warm water— it feels so good. We've all missed him. But we have to wait for him to wake fully. We don't know what a reclaim during unconsciousness would do and none of us care to experiment any further, even Teen Me.*

*My trophy releases a gargling moan and I realize he has eaten through most of his gag.*

'What do you want?' *The officer's voice cracks like a tweenie boy. Okay, let's do this.*

```
Suni: I want to know were my mother
is.

Officer: What?

Suni: My mother. She saved your
wife's life.
```

Officer: My wife is dead.

Suni: You took us from a cave when I was a little girl. My mother is a Mark, a healer, and she promised to heal your wife if you didn't wash me and then you shot your commanding officer. I assume you don't do that very often. You remember me now?

Officer: What are you going to do to me? Please don't make me tell you. You don't understand.

Suni: Do you remember or shall I jog your memory with my fist?

Officer: I remember you. I remember her. I'm so sorry. Look I'll tell you about your mom. I'll tell you whatever I know. Okay? But that's it.

Suni: Where is she?

Officer: She—she said my wife had an infection. A bad one. She said that she could take the infection out but she'd have to put it in someone else. I loved my wife. So much. I had no choice. No choice.

Suni: What are you saying?

Officer: If you had the choice to save someone you loved but had to kill someone to do it, you'd do it too. Everyone would. I had no choice.

Suni: What did you do?

Officer: I told your mother to keep the infection inside her. She didn't want to, she begged. She said she needed to live for her kids. I had no choice. I told her that if she didn't take my wife's infection then I would kill you. I told her she didn't need to live for her kids, she needed to die for them.

Suni: No.

Officer: She did it. Didn't even think about it. She died for you just as fast as I killed for my wife. Okay look, that's all I know. Please let me go. I'm so sorry! I'm sorry!

Axalte: Where did you put her body?

Officer: I told you what I know. Please!

Axalte: No, you are going to sit here until you answer that question. Where did you put her body?

Officer: You don't understand, they'll kill me.

Suni: No, you don't understand that we'll kill you.

Officer: Okay, I don't know where her body is. Right after she took the infection these people, I think they were officers, came and took her. I don't know what they did with her! I promise! I told you everything I know!

*The rest is hazy. Like I don't want to remember it fully. Axalte and Paltino take turns hugging me, followed by empty yet well-meaning self-help phrases like 'at least you know now' and 'at least she lived a full life'. Come to think of it they all started with 'at least'.*

*Axalte goes on interrogating the officer about why he was in that house and who 'they' were. Lute wakes up, Paltino reclaims him and Teen Me tries to appear interested but I know that the reclaim fails and Lute disappears into mind limbo. But none of this matters to me or Teen Me. My mother is dead. She died to save me. My mother is dead. My beautiful mother.*

*When Paltino and Axalte are distracted spewing Lute's life details to him in the hope of bringing him back faster and end up only pushing him further and further into his mental abyss, I grab a dull rock and bludgeon the officer to death.*

# Chapter 29

That wasn't me. I didn't kill him. It was Teen Me. I am not Teen Me. That was not Me, not the real Me. I feel Paltino's hand slip into mine. My eyes open to Axalte's mouth on Joyli's. I want to curl up and crawl into Paltino's hand. Not safe in my mind, not safe out here.

He squeezes my hand. I wish I could hear his voice right now. Paltino, I killed that officer. I gambled with Ms Gord's life. My mother died because of me. Ami died because of me. Fellie, Buzz, Flora, the young officer, the woman in the elevator. I am a monster. All grown up cave monster.

Axalte peels his lips from Joyli's, throws me a cheeseball wink-grin combo and types into his handheld. He's not the real Axalte any more than I'm Teen Me. He must be requesting authorization from The People for our washes. I know Paltino will find me again. They can't wash him. He'll pretend to be washed and come find me. Just like before. He will reclaim me. We will be okay. Paltino and I look at each other. I know he can hear me.

'I don't think so, sugar buns. We know he's a Mark and we don't wash Marks.' Axalte doesn't even pause to see our faces fall. 'And wait a minute. I thought you were in love with me. What's this hand-holding *come find me, I know you will find me* crap?' For this he lobs his arms around in an intentional overdramatic performance.

He can hear my thoughts. How is that possible?

'I think I have given you enough free information for now.' Axalte stares at his handheld. There's no buzzing of handhelds through Pangea, no illumination of plasma screens, which means he did not send a request for authorization to wash. 'Okay, we're good. You're taking him in and I'm taking her.' Axalte slips his handheld away and delivers the message to Joyli. It wasn't a wash. The People did not make that decision. He's taking orders from someone.

'Why are you taking *her* in?' Joyli's cheek pulses as if she is imagining chewing on my bones. The real Joyli is just as gone as the real Axalte.

'Because that's the plan.'

'I don't like the plan.' Joyli's eyes redden like the moon.

'How you feel about it is irrelevant,' Axalte bellows into Joyli's ear and she cowers to her superior. Transmit, receive, process. She pries Paltino's hand from mine.

'Say bye bye to your only friend.' She pouts out her bottom lip and makes a little crybaby face. Without thinking I lift my right foot and kick her in the stomach.

She flies backwards and slams into the wall. Axalte roars out his deep belly laugh, which is becoming increasingly disgusting. I want to destroy this perverse creation, this empty-headed zombie, this mechanized monster, this repulsive, grotesque bastardization of a beautiful man.

'Run, Paltino!' I charge Axalte and punch him in the ribs. He doesn't even flinch but he does stop laughing. With the full force of my body, I thrust the heel of my hand straight up under his nose and push until I hear the snap. Blood gushes from his nose and sprays the floor. Paltino is a few steps from diving out of the window.

Axalte does not even have to move. He just extends his wide arm and grabs Paltino by the hair. I didn't think I could beat him—I thought I could buy Paltino enough time to get out but Axalte is too strong. His eyes ignite in the blue of the rising sun and stare down at me, blood gushing from his nose, and Paltino is shaking in his grasp harder and harder as the current running through him increases in strength.

'Are we done playing?' Axalte's voice is deep and calm. He's terrifying.

'We're done.' I take a step back. Axalte drops Paltino and Joyli hobbles over, trying to hide her injuries. The little bit of Teen Me in me wasn't enough. Axalte realigns his broken nose and pinches it for a few moments until it stops bleeding. He doesn't wipe away the blood that covers his mouth, chin, neck and shirt. He wears it like a badge.

With every movement I brace myself for a hit that doesn't come. The more time passes, the more I anticipate it. He's like a brimming pot on the fire, unstable and about to blow.

Joyli pulls Paltino out of the house. I try to keep my eyes on him but he disappears into a car. Paltino. They know he's a Mark—they are going to drain his powers, transfer his memories, kill him and bury him in a box like Fellie. And just like no one came for Fellie, no one will come for Paltino.

I want to scream but I can't let Axalte see me cry. He's probably listening to my thoughts right now. I don't mind that really. I'd rather him listen to my thoughts than be able to use any of his other powers. Although at this point I'm ready to die. I'm tired.

Axalte takes my arm and struts to his vehicle, flinging me around all the way. At some point I make out Malti hiding in a poppyfly patch. I don't think about her or try to communicate with her. Axalte may be listening. And he speeds off.

We sit in silence until we leave East and are tearing through the barren desert driving farther and farther from any Pangean city.

'What is going to happen to Paltino?'

Axalte slices his neck with a finger and mocks a dead face, tongue wagging and all.

'What's so special about you?' Axalte touches and then tosses a lock of my hair.

'Nothing.'

'Yeah? Then why does The Creator want to see you?'

The Creator? Who's The Creator? Did I know and just didn't remember or did I never know? Does Paltino know? Is that where he's taking me? Axalte barely blinks but when he does, his tight, long, black lashes reach from his eyebrows to the middle of his cheek like flapping wings. The only softness left on his face. I miss him.

'Were we married?'

'We were nothing.'

'Aw, I thought you loved me, sugar lips?'

'The man I love is dead.'

'How disappointing. And here I was thinking this ride might get a bit . . . spicy.' I stare out the window at the vast desert and search for trees to count. 'Well, you wanted freedom. This is freedom. Messy. You want perfection, you should have stayed washed.' My head snaps to him. Those are my words. That's what I said right before I reclaimed Ms Gord. Is he in there still? Axalte?

I shake away the thought. Like a junkie with a bag of drugs in her hand, I have to fight the skin-crawling, muscle-seizing, bone-clammering craving for Axalte.

The real Axalte may have remembered that but he would never have said it. He never believed it. He was the light to my darkness, the morality to my passion, the integrity to my audacity. Together we were balance. Without him I'm a tree without roots, a fish that can't swim, an ornamental carcass, a poisonous lipstick, the blood moon and the carnivorous sun. Without him I am . . . unnatural.

'Damn. You really did love—'

—the back of the car explodes into a cloud of fire, propels up into the air, flips and slams us upside down. Black.

# Chapter 30

*Black. An earthy wet chill. It's a cave. A single match strikes, lighting my mother's face, almost catching a dangle of her hair. She cups her hand around the flickering flame as if it's about to fly away. She lights burnt-down candles that line our cave wall. More and more of her glows with each candle she lights. Her hair is twisted into two messy braids, the hair of a little girl who's been too busy playing to care about it. Shadows fall on her arms, highlighting her defined but sleek muscles. Her old faded dress hugs her tired body. You can barely make out the design. Lilies? Every inch of her is beautiful, down to her unpainted naked perfectly round toes. My beautiful mother. I know that she's gone but to Little Me she's not. She's right there, my living, breathing beautiful mother, immortal in my memories.*

*She opens up a small frayed blanket and drapes a sleeping baby Hayk, tucking in the corners tightly. My bowl of peaches and cream. His mouth hangs open and he snores like an old man. Little Me giggles. Little Me in the red dress (when it still fit) with some meat on her bones. Not a little cave monster, not yet.*

*Little Me scoots to face my mother and passes her a stone bowl of water and a damp cloth. My mother dips the cloth in the water and wipes Little Me's right eye from the nose to the ear. Again. Now the left eye. She places the cloth on my forehead and pulls it down over my nose, my lips and stops at my chin. Again. She continues, slowly, carefully, as this is not just a bath, it's a ritual. This is how my mother loved me.*

*'Mama, who was that man in the forest?' Little Me knows she shouldn't be asking this question but it's been bubbling in her belly for hours and she can't hold it anymore.*

*'Suni, were you following me again?'*

*Little Me drops her head and squeaks out a 'Yes.'*

*'I told you not to do that. It's not safe, my love.' She unbuttons my dress and slips my right arm out of the sleeve. She pulls from the shoulder to the tip of each finger. Her movements are little jerky. She's clearly unhappy with Little Me.*

*'I'm sorry, Mama.' I place my hand on her cheek and she melts into it.*

*'It's okay, sweetie. But don't do it again. There are bad people out there. People who want to take us away from each other with their tricks and their magic. This cave is safe. Caves are safe.' She's not trying to scare Little Me; she's just scared herself. A young mother alone in a cave with her two small children. She knows she can't protect them. She knows she will lose them. And so she glows in each moment, letting the warmth singe her face, holding her breath, knowing she cannot hold this cupped flame forever.*

*'Was he my father?'*

'Don't be silly! No.' My mother hushes her own laugh. 'He was just one of those bad people. The ones we have to hide from. But your father was a good man. Once. And he will come here. He will remember and meet us here.' My mother replaces my arm in my sleeve and slips out my left, pulling the wet cloth from shoulder to each fingertip, careful to scoop under each nail.

'Did he forget us?'

'Yes. But it's not his fault. They made him forget us with their magic—'

'Like witches?' Back straight, eyes wide. Little Me leans in.

'Yes, like witches, and they tricked him into thinking he was someone else. But he will remember and then he will come for us. I know it.'

'How do you know?' Little Me tucks a dangle of my mother's hair behind her ear but it stubbornly springs back out.

'Because I love him. And my love means having faith.'

'Your love? I want my love to mean having lots of bread and swimming every day. And never living in caves.' This sends my mother into a body-shaking laugh that she cannot hush.

'Oh, you will know what your love means when you love someone like I love your father.'

'I love you, and baby Hayk.'

'I know. But this is a different love.' Little Me simmers in the different-kind-of-love thought. How different could it really be? She thinks about how she loves all her paints but especially the blue one. It must be like that.

*It's like imagining what water tastes like if you have never drank it. You don't know until you know and she doesn't know . . . but I do.*

*'I'm going to love like you, Mama. My love is going to mean faith.'*

# Chapter 31

A hand jerks me to the right. My eyes are half open but they don't focus. I'm so tired. That's all I know right now. My eyelids weigh twenty tons and it feels so good to just let them drop. A hand yanks me again and the snap pulls me into clarity . . . somewhat.

I'm upside down in the burning car. Blood trickles from my forehead into my mouth. I don't spit it out; the salty warmth is helping me stay awake, a little. The mostly plastic vehicle melts, dropping blobs of burning plastic. Everything is spinning and I'd still rather be sleeping. Axalte is knocked out and a river of burning plastic edges towards his face. Another long hard pull on my arm. It's Snap and Doltier.

Their mouths flap, veins bulge, arms flail in a silent frenzy. I can't hear them but whatever they are saying seems really important. I chuckle. I'm definitely not okay. Snap is pointing somewhere. Somewhere down in the car. I blink wildly and scrunch my brow trying to concentrate—Paltino-style—and follow his finger down to my leg. Oh! It's snagged on to some sharp thingy. That's why they can't pull me out. I throw my head back and laugh. Snap shakes me out of it. Wait, did he just slap me? Okay. Okay. I'll unsnag my leg. Calm down, boys. And so I do. That was easy.

I'm swooped out of the melty car and flung on to sand in the shade of towering rocks in the shape of a giant 'W'. Malti pours water on to my mouth, eyes and face. I try to smack her away but my movements are uncoordinated and I keep missing her even though she's right on top of me.

'Don't fight me, I need to flush this out of you.' Malti holds my head down and the water floods my nose and my lungs and forces me to roll over and puke. I have thrown up way too many times in the last two days. That's all it's been since this all started? Just two days?

My eyes sharpen into focus and find Snap and Doltier shovelling sand with their hands on the burning plastic that had dripped on to my legs, back and arms. I was burning alive and I didn't even know. The car. The flames rise as the car has all but pooled into a burning lake of plastic. Axalte. I can't bend my right leg—the plastic has now cooled and formed a stiff cast encasing it. I have to get to him. I pull my body towards the burning wreck.

'Stop.' Malti grabs my leg. 'Remember what happened the last time you saved him?'

'If you know that then you must know what happened to the last person who tried to stop me.' I sweep her with my plastic leg and she flies, landing on her back. Snap and Doltier pounce on me.

'Suni, we can't control him. No one can.' Snap tries to soothe me. Not so easy to do when your jiggly belly is on top of me and you're pressing my face in the sand.

'You have a Reclaimer,' I hiss.

'We can't take the risk.' Wiry Doltier is definitely the gentler of the two. I'm not sure if he's being merciful or if he's just weak. I'm guessing a combination of both. His grasp is soft—wispy fingers wrapped around my wrist like a bow on a present, his wobbly knee in the sand rather than in my back and he's using maybe a quarter of his already little strength. His gun grazes my side as he tries to pull my arm behind my back. Pressed against me, I can feel its shape. Large barrel, probably the length of his thigh, thick nozzle. Triple thunder stac .63. Oh, the irony.

I can wriggle free one finger—just one—from his grip and reach the trigger. Well, Ms Gord, I guess the single-finger trigger was not a useless feature after all. Without hesitation I fire not knowing which way the gun is facing, whether it will fire nowhere or hit Doltier, Snap, Malti or me.

It hits Doltier in the leg and he falls off me, leaving the gun in my grasp. He shouldn't have underestimated me. Snap looks at Doltier for just a millisecond, just enough time for me to shove the barrel of the triple thunder stac .63 up under his chin. I look over at Doltier. How badly did I hit him? He tears his pant leg open. It's just a graze. Enough to scare them but not enough to hurt him. I exhale a little but don't let them see it. I have to act like Teen Me. I have to be Teen Me.

'Now listen up. I am going to pull Axalte out and if any one of you tries to stop me I will blow every last one of you away.' Snap throws up his hands. I can feel Teen Me burning through my chest—sexy, spunky, cheeky, strong, fearless, passionate, murdering Teen Me. It's intoxicating, it's relieving, it's comfortable. I'm not comfortable with how comfortable I am with this.

Malti speaks, chalky and airy, still chasing her breath. 'Let her go, you heard Paltino, Snap. Let her go.' I want to laugh at the absurdity of the notion that they or anyone can 'let' me do anything. I am holding the gun. They are not letting me go, I am letting *them* go. But there's no time to deal with this right now. Axalte's time is slipping away and I won't lose him to anything let alone my ego.

I slog to the wreckage and can barely see Axalte's face through a closing window. His body is all but covered in burning plastic. I reach my hands in and pull, but the plastic has further weighted his already massive body. I feel my cheek heat up and sting. Some plastic must have flung on to it. No, it's the sun. My sunsafe must have worn off.

I dig my heels into the sand and lean back into the pull. I pull him just inches before I see Snap, Doltier and Malti pulling along beside me. A few heaves and he's out.

Sand pats out his burns but leaves him almost in a full body cast of cool hardened plastic. Only his face, neck, right chest and arm are exposed. He opens his eyes for a moment and looks at me. They are his eyes. His sparkly-twinkly-almond eyes. His eyebrows tilt up in the centre and his lips open into a plump and meaty smile. With his free hand he traces a line from my eyebrow to my chin. He's with me. It's Axalte. Then his eyes close and he slips away again.

'Axalte! I know you're there. Axalte!'

'It's not him.' Malti places her hand on my shoulder. My reflex is to slap it away but I don't. I need to feel the warmth of a friend. 'It's the chemical in the fumes from the repurposed plastic. It makes you loopy. You were laughing while you were burning alive.' She's right. But that still means he's in there somewhere, buried deep in the loopy parts of him. Doesn't it? Yes, it does. My love means faith. He's in there.

My cheek is now smoking in the sun. Malti pulls me into the shade and the boys drag Axalte behind us. They struggle in the sand. Covered in plastic, his body is as heavy as a car.

'Is Toke okay? And you can connect with Paltino? Is he okay?' I ask.

'Toke's fine.' Malti searches her zippered pockets for something. 'Paltino is alive, for now. We were going to get him. But he wanted us to get you first.'

'Let's move, then.'

'Not yet. I'll tell you when.' She finally pulls out some helder leaves and passes them to Doltier but I intercept them and place them on my tongue.

Blood drips from where I grazed him. I want to say I am sorry but I'm not. Apologies are self-serving anyway and it wouldn't mean anything. I'd do it again to save Axalte. They all know that. But I pour water over his wound and wrap it in the helder leaves soaked in my saliva. This is my apology.

'I was the one who planted the bomb in the car. I may have overdone it with the explosives. So I guess we are even now.' Doltier half smiles and passes me his sunsafe. This is him accepting my apology. I use it while I think of Axalte's stressed-out sunsafe commandments and the kiss that followed.

Malti passes me a knife and I slice open the plastic cast on my leg. I jimmy it off but lose some patches of my skin that it had melded into. The remaining skin is burnt or blistered. But I can't really feel any pain. All I can think about is that Axalte must have this all over his body. And then I notice why Snap and Malti have been so quiet. They have searched Axalte's exposed pockets and pulled out a narrow case of syringes. The doses.

They are talking to each other in their minds, I can see it. Arms moving, hands gesturing to Axalte and me and a lot of nodding.

'What are you doing?' I accuse.

'We have to get Paltino.' Malti points to a car behind the 'W' rock formation that I had not even noticed. 'This isn't going to be easy, and you and Doltier are wounded.'

'And Axalte.' Why is she forgetting him?

'Yeah and Axalte. There's a healer dose in here. I'm going to administer it to him and then put his hand on both of you to heal you.' That's it? I was expecting something more ominous. That's not all of it. It can't be. Malti fingers the back of her neck uncomfortably. 'We have to reclaim him. If he wakes he'll take us all down. I know you already know that.'

'You can't reclaim him now while he's unconscious and under the influence of that chemical. We don't know what that can do to him. He may not survive it. He's in the cast. He won't be able to move if he wakes.'

'When we give him the healer dose, he will heal himself. And when he wakes he will be able to break out of this cast in seconds. I can't gamble with Paltino's life but I can gamble with his.' Malti lowers her gaze and draws an 'O' in the sand with her foot. 'I'm sorry, we knew you would resist.'

Doltier stabs a syringe into my neck. 'It's just going to put you to sleep. And now we're even.'

My arms flail and my right hand grabs a hold of Doltier's hair ripping a fistful out. Too late . . . he's already emptied the syringe into my neck. Fuzzy. The world is blurring. Snap rushes over to me. I think I am fighting. Fists in the air. Kicking and landing wherever I can reach. I grab and squeeze and pull whatever is in my hands. The light goes out and comes back in small flashes. I have a gun in my hand and I'm firing everywhere. I think I hear a faint screaming hidden in the skull-banging hum that forces all other sound out of my head. My hair flies in and out of my eyes and I catch a glimpse of me blowing off half of the 'W' rock, watching it somersault through the air and flatten the car, our only way out, into a pancake.

# Chapter 32

'Flattened into a pancake?' I swipe at a dimmer Teen Paltino, as worn as the now Paltino. Teen Me pokes him in the shoulder. 'Can you be any more insensitive?' Paltino rubs his poked shoulder and half smiles, half frowns.

'But that's what happened. The machine depressurized, snapped and flat-crushed them.' Axalte's parents. Both dead. Factory accident.

We are treading down the Pangean street, our heels hitting the ground so hard every other word bursts a little louder than the one before. We need to get out of there fast. We were supposed to reclaim them in just a few days. Just a few days.

Paltino jabbers on about how 'at least they didn't suffer' and 'at least they died together'. Enough with the 'at leasts'. It's not like Axalte and I piled those on Paltino when he lost Lute to the mental limbo. If you think hard enough you can see a silver lining on every cloud. That's why they don't mean anything. Sometimes when you're mourning you don't want to think of the brighter side, the meaning, the purpose of it all. Sometimes you just want to cry and cry and cry.

There he is. Axalte sits on the ground in front of a bright wild poppyfly field. In the wild they are multicoloured like giant bowls of candies, each one slightly different than the other but also the same.

I curl up next to Axalte, pulling my knees to my chest. His back is straight, legs crossed, eyebrows knitted and lips pressed into a line. This is the Real Axalte—angry. We both sit and watch waves of poppyflies take flight only to die and then drift back down as empty carcasses. I slip my hand in his and we sit amidst the colourful death for as long as he needs.

'I have no idea who they were. The real them, the unwashed them,' Axalte speaks out to the field as if he is addressing the universe, not just me. 'It's fake, everything is fake during the wash. But it doesn't make sense. I loved them. How can it be fake if I loved them?' This question is for me but I don't have an answer and I can't tell him what he wants to hear. I would be lying.

'Just promise me one thing, Suni. If I'm washed and you can't reclaim me promise me that you'll kill me.'

Teen Me stares out into the field thinking she knows her answer. But like Little Me trying to imagine what love is, Teen Me can't imagine what killing that love would be. You don't know until you know. He pulls me in close and buries his face in my hair as if to inhale me.

'I promise,' I say.

# Chapter 33

My mouth flies open. I gulp air. Jittery electricity twitches through my scalp and scampers to my toes. Then I feel the heat of the needle in my neck and I'm up. Adrenaline.

All three of them are on top of me. Snap, Doltier and Malti. I don't even know who's holding the syringe but as soon as I can breathe I free my hand, pull the syringe out of my neck and stick it in whoever's knee was pushing down on my chest—Malti's. She yowls and recoils off me. I have no burns on my skin. I have been healed, which means that they gave Axalte a dose and probably reclaimed him too. If anything has happened to him I will tear them apart. My jaw locks and I scream through my teeth.

'Suni, stop. We woke you because he's okay, Axalte is awake.' I freeze. Snap and Doltier crawl off me and I see him, just a few feet away from me. Eyes twinkly, shoulders slouched, softer, gentler Axalte. My Axalte. He's healed and the plastic is gone. He is just sitting there, straight-backed, legs crossed and lips pressed into a line.

I climb into his wide arms. He wraps around me, buries his nose into my hair as if to inhale me and for the first time in as long as I can remember I feel safe.

'How much do you remember?' I whisper.

'Not much. But I remember us in that poppyfly field. That's enough.' I slurp up his honey voice.

'That was my first memory, too.' He cocoons me in a woody embrace and I lose myself in him to the point that I forget where we are, what has happened and what has not.

'We have to get Paltino. We don't have much time.' Axalte scoots me off and rises, towering over everyone else, casting a shadow as long and wide as the 'W'— now 'V' rock. I dig my thumb into that hole in my pant leg as I recall that I shot the rock and crushed the car.

'Well, we can't do that anymore now, can we?' Snap, having lost all his jolly, barks. I can see Malti shut him up in his mind. I don't know why she is defending me, this is my fault. I did this and I deserve that bark and even a bite, too.

'I'm not defending you. We should have just been more careful. Paltino said you were fire. Uncontrollable, unpredictable fire. It's our fault that we let him down.' Malti chokes on her words. 'We don't have a way out. There's no tunnel system out here, no vehicles and we can't make it back in the sun, we don't have enough sunsafe. We will have to wait it out here in the shade until nightfall.' Her voice trails off to a breathless whisper. She knows what that means.

'He'll be dead by then.' Axalte's vein pulses in his neck. He's angry. The real him never showed anger like this. The reclaim brings back your washed memories but it doesn't erase what you were during the wash. You have these two versions of you: who you were before the wash and who you were during the wash. Like two demons in your belly constantly fighting for possession of your soul; you have to learn to control them and unleash the right one at the right time because you can never rid yourself of either demon. Who you were is gone. This is who you are now. This is the only salvation we have.

'There may not be enough sunsafe for all of us to make it but there's enough for one of us.' I can't let Paltino die. Not like this. Not because of me.

'You don't understand. He doesn't have time. They have already taken him to the lab. They will extract his memories, his Mark and then kill him. He's got one hour, maybe two. That's it. You can't get there,' Axalte growls. The new Axalte is just like Teen Me. But if that is who he is now then we have lost our balance.

'He's dead already then,' Doltier whines and withdraws to the furthest shaded part against the rock.

'Not yet. Where are my doses?' Axalte orders.

'Why?' Even in the shade Malti's sharp cheeks hide her sunken face in dark shadows.

'I have a teleport dose in there. I can take the shot, teleport into the lab, grab him and teleport back here . . . the whole thing will take seconds.'

'Okay, I will go with you.' There's no way I'm letting him out of my sight.

'I can only transport one person at a time. I need to go alone so that I can bring him back.'

'What if you don't come back?' Malti bites.

'Why wouldn't I come back?

'What if the reclaim didn't take? You've been washed for a long time. And this whole time you could've just been faking it, trying to find a way to get to your doses because you knew that's the only way out of here for you.' Malti has been thinking this the whole time.

'He's not pretending. He remembered the poppyfly field. He had a memory, That means the reclaim worked,' I snarl at Malti. I can feel Teen Me boiling up my throat.

'We don't have time for this. Paltino doesn't have time for this.' Axalte narrows his eyes and drops his brow. The Commander is boiling up his throat.

'Yeah, I agree.' Malti pulls the syringe out of her pocket and plunges it into her thigh. She empties a third of it in before she slumps on the ground, seizing, sending her body pummelling through the sand. The syringe juts out of her thigh.

We rush to her. 'Malti!' Her eyes roll to white as her limbs and fingers gnarl into knots and release to slam into anything around and tighten back into deformed shapes. Her tight bun unravels, pouring her fiery red hair over the sand. 'What's happening to her?'

'Not just anyone can take a dose. You have to have the gene,' Axalte answers what we should have already known. I read that in the headquarters. We should have known. Her hanging tongue flaps around her face and I try to hold her head still but it's slick with sweat and pops out of my fingers like a slippery ice cube and she bites off her own tongue in two blood-spraying chomps. Her tongue slaps around in the sand like a chipfin.

That's when I notice Axalte with the syringe in his hand. I didn't even see him taking it out of Malti's leg. That's right, Axalte. We don't have time. You go get Paltino. I'll stay with her.

He throws a cocksure wink-grin combo at me as he injects himself with remainder of the dose. 'Stupid, stupid Seggie.'

Everything plunges deep into the sand below me— my gut, my arms, my jaw, my skin, everything pulling, sinking, shrivelling, recoiling, dissipating until there is nothing. There is nothing left.

'But you remembered. You remembered the poppyfly field. How you sat there, how you breathed me in.' The words break on my gagging throat.

'I was reading your mind when you had that memory, sugar lips.' My mother's voice scratches at my skull as

Snap and Doltier charge him. He flicks one into the 'V' rock and swats the other into the sun. *'There are bad people out there . . . bad people with their tricks and their magic.'*

He tugs me into his side and wraps one arm around my waist like a hero would hold his damsel. 'Now hold on, sexy. There's someone just dying to meet you.'

# Chapter 34

*The poppyfly field.*

*'Just promise me one thing, Suni. If I'm washed and you can't reclaim me, promise me that you'll kill me.' Axalte pulls Teen Me in close and buries his face in my hair as if to inhale me.*

*'I promise.'*

*Why am I back here? At this memory? What is Teen Me trying to tell me? I cannot do it. I cannot kill him. It's him. It's Axalte even though it's not Axalte. It's his honey voice, his deep belly laugh, his girlie-lashed almond eyes. I cannot fight him. I have nothing left in me. It's all gone. Ami, Fellie, Flora, Buzz, Malti, my mother, my brother, Paltino and Axalte. I have lost them all, there is no fight left in me. I'm broken and I just want to sleep. There is nothing left in me. I am not you, Teen Me. The wash diluted you with . . . me. Me and my empathy, me and my corrosive guilt, me and my hollow ache, me and my solitude. You had everyone, Teen Me, and I lost everyone. I am not sexy, cheeky, spunky, smart you. I am guilty, hollow, lonely, broken me.*

'Well, aren't you going to ask me?' Teen Me pulls out of Axalte's hold and knees to chest, rocks back and forth. Ear-to-ear smile, like she's got something to say.

'Okay, so if you've been washed and I can't reclaim you what would you want me to do?' Axalte asks.

'I'd want you to reclaim me.'

'Yeah, but I can't.'

'Figure it out.'

'I can't, that's the whole point.'

'You're asking me what I'd want and I'd want you to find a way.' Teen Me tilts up her chin and barely looks at him through the corner of her eyes. Sexy, cheeky, spunky Teen Me. Axalte sucks his teeth and eyeballs her. He lets his straight back roll into a relaxed slouch and he even cracks a half smile.

'Oh, okay. So just figure it out! Just like that!' He waves his hands around in a 'do as I say' way as he mocks Teen Me's voice in an over-shrill, over-commanding tone. On another day that would have got Axalte a few shoulder pokes and possibly a flip but not today. Teen Me just wants to make sure he doesn't return to that dark place where he was when she first found him at this field.

'Yeah. Just like that.'

'Oh, so you'd kill me but you want me to find a way to save you?' he scoffs.

'No, you said that if you were washed and I couldn't reclaim you, then to kill you.'

'Yeah . . .'

'So I promised because I know that would never happen. I would find a way to reclaim you. I would figure it out. I know I would. Just like I know you would. We'd find each other and save each other. Always. I know that because I love you and my love means faith.' Teen Me dramatically drapes herself over his shoulder and swoons like a damsel in the arms of her hero.

I am not you, Teen Me.

# Chapter 35

Axalte squeezes me to him a little tighter and his hand slips a little lower than necessary. Malti's violent seizing has calmed into a slow shiver and white foam seeps from her mouth. Snap scrambles hard for the shade as he covers his face with his arms, which are smoking in the sun. I can smell his flesh burning—it smells the same as Fellie's did. I can't even see where Doltier is.

Then the teleportation begins. First it's a funny feeling in the pit of your stomach, like someone is in there tickling your belly with a feather. Then it turns into a tug at your gut, as if that someone is crushing his heavy hands into your intestines and dragging them down into the ground. Pulling and ripping you apart inside out, your lungs, each vein, cracking your bones, tearing your skin. But it's fast. So fast that I don't have a chance to scream . . . and it's over.

Axalte loosens his grip on my waist but clamps on to my wrist. I can't see anything but him. Everything is black, as if we are in a giant coffin but for the one blinding light that shines on us both from above and dims before it illuminates the ground. It's just us from the waist up floating in blackness. There's something about this blackness that feels huge and makes me feel tiny.

There's someone else here. I can't see him or hear him but I can feel his eyes on me. Examining me, judging me, counting my flaws, subtracting my weaknesses and summing me up.

'Hello, Suni.' His voice is not deep but loud, full of bass and comes from all directions, as if it's not a human voice but a speaker—a lot of speakers. Axalte lowers his head in some sort of a bow and when he notices that I don't, he forces my head down. 'Do you know who I am?'

I raise my head back up. I am not bowing. I know I'm dying here and I'm not dying bowing. I should want to know who he is and why he's doing this. Why is he hiding? Why does he kill Marks? Why convince The People that they rule themselves? What is the purpose of all of this? But I don't ask anything. I just want to die. Quickly.

'Aren't you the least bit curious as to why I wanted to see you?' The Creator is playing with me.

'I think you want me to be. I think you want to tell me about what you've done and why you've done it. But you know what? I don't care.' Silence fills the black room for what feels like a very long time. Axalte doesn't move out of his bow. A drop of sweat makes its way from the back of his neck to his chin and dangles for a bit before it falls into the blackness.

The Creator, or whatever he is, wants something from me, that's why I am here. And if he wants something then that means I have leverage. I just have to figure out how to use it.

'Okay, I'll play your game.' With my free hand I twist up my hair and rest the black, messy tornado on my shoulder. 'If you let Paltino live.'

'Paltino? Not Axalte?'

I look at Axalte, head hanging in his unbreakable bow, girlie-lashed eyes closed, sunken face. 'Axalte is dead.'

'Fine. Paltino lives. If you answer two questions for me.'

Questions? What could I possibly know that he doesn't? Axalte has been in my mind for hours; he could tell him whatever he knows. He is probably listening to my thoughts right now.

'He's not. That dose ran out just a few minutes ago. But I am listening. I have always been listening. This mind-reading gift is a bit of a double-edged sword. I can hear your thoughts but just what you are thinking right now. I cannot go rummaging around in your brain to find what I want. It's quite frustrating. But face-to-face is a different story. I don't need your permission to get you to answer anything. I was really just letting you think you had control when I accepted your deal. It's amazing how far a sense of autonomy goes, even if it is fake.' He pauses for a moment as if to let me think about what he just said. He's talking about the washes and The People. The People have never been in control of anything. We have never had a choice. He just gave us a false sense of control while he pulled all the strings and tricked us into believing he doesn't exist. *'There are bad people out there . . . with their tricks and their magic.'*

I'm not going to tell you anything. No matter what you say, no matter what you do, you cannot make me answer you. You have taken everything there is to take from me. You have no leverage because I have nothing to lose. And you, hiding here in the dark like a criminal, forced into a self-made prison of solitude, drunk with the power you have stolen. You are no more than a common thug. A thug with magic tricks. Nothing more.

'I am The Creator,' he bellows. The depth of the bass of his mechanized voice bangs in my skull. 'I saved you all. Out of the ashes of The Cleanse, on the bones of millions dead, I built Pangea. I gave you all the principles, the foundation of a stable society of inclusion, where we are equal, we are all one, united we stand, divided we fall. There are no murders, no crimes, no theft, no racism, no sexism, no classism, nobody thinks they are better than anyone else because of what God they pray to. I have built this world. I have. I am The Creator.' His voice loudens with each word until it reaches a painful ringing level that forces Axalte to cover his ears without dropping my wrist. I cup one ear and press the other into my shoulder. The ringing pierces my head like thin, long needles. When he stops we slowly remove our hands.

Is this what he wants? To gloat? For me to congratulate him on his brilliant plan? For me to thank him for his graciousness?

'It's not real. It's fake. There are crimes, murders, theft, racism, sexism . . . all of it. You just wash it away so no one remembers. But it's all still there. You haven't saved anyone, you trapped everyone in prisons in their minds, like you've trapped yourself here,' I snarl around the blackness.

'You are boring me. How did you remember Axalte during your wash?'

This is what he wants to ask me? I don't know the answer to that. Why does he care? What difference does it make? Who cares about me and Axalte? I hang my head when I realize I just answered his question.

'Where is your mother?'

'My mother? Axalte and my mother? The gigantic all-knowing Creator does not even know the answer to these small questions? What is this, some perverse fascination with my misery? What am I, entertainment to you? Well, I hate to break it to you but they are dead. Both of them. Axalte and my mother are dead and you killed them both. I answered your questions, now let Paltino go.'

'No. I want Paltino to die.'

'Why?'

'Because you don't.' He laughs a little. He finds this fun, like a kid chucking chipfins in the sun just to watch them sizzle to their deaths.

'Show your face. Show your face, you coward!'

Axalte punches me in the jaw. My head snaps to the side and two teeth fly out of my mouth.

'Commander, you did not take a full dose of teleportation. You will have just one complete jump left. When you reach the lab, re-dose. After this girl is extracted I want you to bring me her heart. I'm going to eat it while it's still beating in my hand.'

'I hope you choke on it,' I hiss.

Axalte pulls me to his side. 'Yes, sir.' I'm going to die now, finally. I'm ready. I'm tired. I pull in closer to Axalte and bring my lips to his ear. Apologies mean nothing. They are self-serving and explanations are just excuses. But I need this apology. I need to say it, for me.

'I'm so sorry, Axalte. I failed you. I could not save you. I could not reclaim you and I could not kill you. I broke my promise to you, my love.' I press my bloody lips on to his as the teleport begins tugging, ripping, pulling us apart inside out.

# Chapter 36

My shoes click-clack on the white, shiny floors of the white, shiny hallway. It's Teen Me bottled up in a suit, pulled and stretched into a bun, pretending to be contained and controlled. Officers, Experts and Administrators scurry by in an orderly fashion on their way to complete their assigned tasks post-haste. Transmit, receive, process. I'm in the belly of the beast. Headquarters.

I pause at the cluster of bobbleheads collected by the water cooler. Did you see the movie yesterday? This morning's sandstorm was a real doozy! Ooh, love the new hairstyle. Smile, nod and throw in a periodic chuckle. Wait, isn't there usually one more bobblehead in this cluster?

'Ti.' Bobblehead Senior whispers her name. The cluster leans in, I follow. 'She was redistributed. I heard that she had unauthorized, well you know, with that new maintenance worker from the fourth floor. You know the new one with the long hair? He's gone too.' Regurgitate the recycled reaction: Gasp, clutch chest, appear concerned but not mournful and use phrases that begin with 'at least', that is, at least they redistributed her before she got pregnant.

Unauthorized potential procreation. The People boast that every Pangean is free to love whom they choose. The law is not really about the sex, it's about the baby. It's not about morality, it's about integration. It's not about emotion, it's about duty. It's about ensuring the most diverse crossing of genes to breed out diversity. So any extramarital or premarital activities that can't lead to a pregnancy are not prohibited. Homosexuality is not illegal—just as long as one fulfills one's duty to procreate with a blood match, one can do whatever they want on the side. So it's not about love. Pangea lets you love whoever you want to love. But you just can't be with them. It's like The Creator said, it's the illusion of control, the illusion of choice, the illusion of freedom.

Teen Me makes a mental note: Reclaim Ti.

Someone says something that everyone laughs at and so I join in and find the right time to make my exit. You wouldn't think it would be so hard to act ordinary. Even Teen Me has to admit that you can't help but envy the simplicity of their lives. A few empty greetings delivered in plastic smiles later, I am back at my desk.

Ti. Search the central mainframe for all washes in East in the last twenty-four hours. Nothing. Last forty-eight hours. There we go. Ti. Redistribution complete. Assigned as a border guard in North. Her picture loads up on the plasma. Teen Me doesn't think anything of it but I do. I know her face. It's Malti.

A Pangean alert rings through the system, on handhelds and pulls up on all plasmas. It's Axalte's face with the word RISER stamped across it. Interfered with wash of unidentified girl. Immediate wash on capture AUTHORIZED.

All my blood floods into my chest, inflating my heart. I can feel it in my temples thumping, banging, stomping, drowning. Be resourceful, Suni.

There's no time. There's no point trying to remove the alert. It's already been transmitted through the mainframe to every terminal. I cannot modify anything that's already been locally distributed. An internal communication flashes from an officer with Axalte's location. I intercept the communication before it's transmitted through the mainframe. East pavilion auditorium. I disable the officer's handheld. This will buy us a few minutes maybe. Amidst the mobs of officers running here and there in response to the alert, I zip down the hallway, the stairs and out of the building. East pavilion auditorium. I keep repeating it in my head like a chant just in case Paltino didn't hear it the first time. East pavilion auditorium. How could he have let himself be revealed like this? East pavilion auditorium. Sexy, spunky, cheeky Teen Me knows she's going to save him. But I know this is where I lose him. I am not Teen Me.

I can see the rear entry to the East pavilion auditorium. Three officers group, in helmets and bullet proof vests, guns out, ready to make a move. Their heads whip to my clickety-clackety shoes. Transmit, receive, process. I am an Expert; they rise and bow their heads in respect.

'The Riser scum is in there?' I sound official.

'Yes, he's in on the left. Damn guy is alone and has taken out four officers already,' one of them discloses. Doesn't matter which one as they are all interchangeable different physical versions of the same person; Teen Me may not know who, but I do—The Creator.

Axalte took out four officers already? That means they are scared of him. They don't wash what they are afraid of.

'Do we have anyone on the exit points?' I slip two Washers out of my holster and into my hands.

'Yes, we have three in the front and two on the side. We were finally able to get a communication into headquarters and we should have more officers in a matter of minutes.' The officers ready their weapons. They don't have Washers out. They don't wash what they fear, they kill what they fear. They gesture to follow in a single file as they approach the door.

I pull the officer in front of me by the collar so that he flings back into my chest and shove the Washer into his tear duct and squeeze. By the time he releases a yelp and the next officer turns to me I already have the Washer spraying into his eye but not before his one finger on the trigger of his triple thunder stac .63 spasms and fires, blowing up a collection of trash cans a hundred feet away. This single-finger trigger will haunt me forever.

After the last officer and I watch the garbage flutter through the air and land he shuffles around and stares at me for a long time. It's Buzz. He tries to look past the barrel of the gun I pulled out at some point and shoved in his face.

'Are you a Riser?' His voice is deep but wobbly. Teen Me nods without blinking. 'Are you going to kill me?' Teen Me shakes her head. 'Why not?' He almost sounds disappointed.

'Because you're a Mark.' Teen Me lowers the gun and pulls out the Reclaimer.

'No, I'm not.'

Teen Me slips off Buzz's helmet and reaches up to rest her hand on his angled face. His blue eyes sizzle and all his meaty muscles unclench just a bit.

'You don't have to hide it anymore.' Teen Me pushes the Reclaimer to his brow and shields her eyes from the flash of light. His giant body lightens as he collapses in her grasp. She rests him up against the wall. I reclaimed you, you reclaimed me. Teen Me saved you for me to let your meaty hands slip through my fingers like silk into the grey poisonous fog that swallowed you forever.

Had I washed you today instead of reclaiming you, would you still be alive? Teen Me's freedom is messy, risky. She doesn't know what that means. She hasn't lost everyone, yet. But she will and then she will wonder what it was all for. Maybe The Creator was right. Maybe the illusion of choice is enough if it means survival. What is the point of having choice, freedom, love when you lose it all in the end anyway?

More officers dart around a building corner and charge for the auditorium. One hundred feet away? Maybe fifty? I have seconds, maybe a minute before they are in the auditorium, guns blazing. I storm through the doors. Three officers guns aimed at Axalte stand frozen, not firing, not talking, not moving, not even blinking. They just hold their positions like statues. Axalte has a strange look in his eyes, something I have never seen before, the black of his pupil stretched open like a hungry mouth that has all but eaten the gentle almond-brown of his iris. It's fear. He's afraid. A little girl peeks at me from around his leg.

Her long, oily hair is stiff and matted, and branches down her shoulders to well below her waist. Her pasty and sunken face is blue in some places and green in others, like a corpse. Yet, her fat cracked lips curve into a little smile, exposing her brown teeth chiselled to sharp points like an animal. Feral wild child. She steps out from behind Axalte but clings to his leg. Her dress is several sizes too small but looks like it must have been pretty once. I know this girl. I knew who this girl was once. I pull out the sketch the border guard gave me when we crossed cities to find Paltino. Not that I have to. Her face is imprinted in my mind. I never forgot that face. The plump cheeks, the ringlets of hair, the fat lips. This is the ghost of that girl.

How long has she lived out there, alone, hiding, scared. How much did she lose of herself to survive? What did she kill and eat? How much garbage fills her belly? How long has it been since she was hugged? She doesn't take her eyes off of me. Feral wild child, meet little cave monster. I know why Axalte risked himself to save her; she is me, I am her, and he made a promise.

She's a Mark. She's frozen those officers. Axalte scoops her up in his arms and washes each frozen officer, one at a time. We don't have time. Those other officers must have reached by now. We have to get out of here. More and more officers will just keep coming and coming. We can't wash them all. I toss Axalte a weapon and we cower behind a row of seats just as we hear the doors click open. Feral wild child snuggles into Axalte. She missed being held.

I inch down until I'm flat on my belly and squint through the rows and rows of seat legs. Ten officers. We can't do this. Feral wild child, can you hear me? Her eyes open and she nods. Can you freeze them like you did the others? She shrugs her shoulders to her ears. No one has taught her to use her powers, she doesn't know what she's capable of. No time to learn now. I snake back down and watch three of the officers freeze in their spots. Just three of the ten. The others start screaming and firing everywhere. One shot ricochets off the wall and snipes into Axalte's leg. He bites his lip and pounds his fist on the ground. He can't scream or they'll know where we are.

Through the seat legs, cool gun pressed up against my hot cheek, blinking sweat from my eyes, I aim at an officer's foot and fire. The officer thuds to the ground. Now, I have a clear shot to her head. She yelps and clutches her foot. She's just a kid, a few years older than feral wild child, the same age as me. The same age as the young soldier I killed with my kiss. Does she really deserve to die? Do any of them? How many die for this revolution? Teen Me doesn't pause to think about it. She takes out two more officers the same way. I wish I could close my eyes so I don't have to watch her—me—kill. In the end I know that they all die for nothing. All of them. Ami, Buzz, Malti, the woman in the elevator, the young soldier, Lute, Paltino and

Axalte. They all die for nothing because we lose and The Creator wins. I want to roar to Teen Me to stop. Stop killing and stop fighting, there's no point. But this is a memory and what's done is done.

Three officers frozen, three dead, there should be four more but I can't see any more feet. They must have jumped up on the seats. I have no idea where they are and I can hear them getting closer and closer.

Feral wild child puts her light-like-a-leaf hand on my shoulder and I just let it rest there, careful not to move and careful not to blow it away. She quivers out of Axalte's arms and into mine. Her body is so tiny and thin I am afraid to hold her back; she would just crumple. She coils into a bony ball and burrows into me. Just a scared little girl. I will protect you. I won't let them hurt you. You are safe now. You will never be alone again, feral wild child. She closes her sunken eyes and rests her head on my chest. Axalte traces a line from my eyebrow to my chin. He's with me. This is the last memory I will have before I die and this is where I lose him.

The officers are close. Their boots clunk on each seat. One row away. I ready my weapon. Four of them, two of us. We can do this. We have to do this—

The door to the auditorium swings open, followed by the loud thuds of one, two, three, four officers hitting the ground. We peek over the seats. Paltino. I knew you would make it, Paltino.

He washes the frozen officers and Axalte dashes over to help. We have got to get out of here now but they have to be washed *first. Paltino and my identities are still unknown to The People. We need to maintain our Pangean access especially now that Axalte has revealed himself and will have to go into hiding in Una. If only Teen Me knew how pointless all this was.*

*I bounce on my toes as if the rocking will soothe feral wild child. Her eyes are still closed and she's snug as a bug. She trusts me. She knows I will protect her. How long has it been since she has trusted herself to someone else? I push her oily hair from her face. Pretty little monster—*

*—a bullet flies into her chest.*

*Feral wild child's black gaping eyes spring open as blood bubbles out of her mouth and her eyelids drop. I fall on to my knees and rock the tiny lifeless body. Axalte and Paltino take down the barely alive officer who fired out his last shot before his last breath as I howl for feral wild child as Fellie howled for Flora.*

*Apologies are self-serving but I need this. I need to say this, for me. I am sorry I could not protect you. I am sorry I could not save you. I am sorry I broke my promise to you. This world is not made for you, feral wild child, as this world was not made for me, little cave monster. There is a better place for you. I will see you there.*

*I kiss one sunken cheek. Lips gluey with her blood, I kiss her other sunken cheek.*

# Chapter 37

I want to stay in the bloody kiss with Axalte even if it is forced on him. Tears pour out of the corners of my closed eyes. Tears for the chipfin, the missing trees, Buzz, Ami, Malti, feral wild child, little cave monster, Axalte, my mother, my brother, Paltino. But not for me, I don't cry for me.

When I open my eyes we are in the lab in the headquarters. Axalte doesn't remove his arm from my waist—proud to tote his trophy. Hunters prowl through the empty gurneys draped with swinging straps that clang and echo the wails of the Marks that died there. One Mark left—Paltino. He's strapped in, eyes closed, not moving. Please don't be dead, Paltino. Let me die first. I can't bear another loss. I am not strong enough.

Joyli flings herself on to Axalte and spews words of longing and worry dripping with the most annoying kind of affection. The kind that makes me scoff and roll my eyes. They have a bizarre conversation about the kiss and

Axalte spends a lot of time reassuring her of his love for her. Even with all these powers and the wash she's still insecure. But she's not the real Joyli any more than Axalte is the real Axalte. So I can laugh at her silliness and dream of killing her in different ways. She curls her lips back over her teeth and perches on Axalte's hip. Well, I can dream for the next few minutes of my life.

'It's not like he pulled away or anything.' I sprinkle some salt on her wound and seal it with a wink-grin combo—Axalte style. If I'm going to die, I'm going to die like Teen Me would have wanted to. Springing from Axalte's hip she pounces on me, fills both fists with my hair and pounds my head into the ground. Axalte rips her off me and she flies into a few empty gurneys. I can still feel the clanging in my brain.

'Why is she not sedated?' Joyli snarls.

'I have specific orders for her. Now control yourself or I will have to.' Axalte points his finger down in her face. 'My doses were taken by Risers. I need yours.'

'I don't have any left. None of us do. We have to wait for the new batch to be released. It's against protocol to have her in here and not sedated.' Joyli gushes at Axalte and growls at me, switching back and forth in a freakish schizophrenic way. I don't even care. Just kill me and get it over with.

Axalte pushes against Joyli and she wilts in his glare, as she wilted in Toke's hold. 'Do I need to remind you of your rank, Legionnaire?'

Transmit, receive, process. She shakes her head and retracts. Axalte pulls me as he stomps over to Paltino. 'Has he been extracted?' Other Hunters confirm that Paltino is up next. He's still alive. Paltino. My sweet friend. You have always been there when I needed you. From when you came to broken, lost Little Me lying in the dirt, to when you reined in sexy, spunky, cheeky Teen Me to when you pulled scared, alone me out of Fellie's coffin. I have always needed you to protect me—all the versions of me, Paltino. I have always needed you.

'Excellent,' Axalte jitters. 'Let's have some fun first, shall we?' Axalte unstraps Paltino from his gurney. He wraps both hands around Paltino's neck and squeezes but watches me with thirsty eyes. He wants me to see this. It's almost as if he's anticipating something from me. I can't play games anymore. I'm done. Joyli breathes in loud grunts and runs her hands along the wall, seething with excitement like a caged animal smelling dinner on its way. I want to cry but I think I may already be crying. Paltino's face bulges with blood and begins to turn blue. He's dying.

'If there is any part of you that is still human, please, kill me first.' I am tired. I cannot do this anymore. I have nothing left.

'No. I am going to kill him first. Now you tell me, are you going to just sit there and watch him die?'

# Chapter 38

Axalte slips the lifeless feral wild child from my arms and pulls me into his. I burrow into him as she did. The auditorium is littered with the bodies of officers we killed and the washed officers fuddle around in their blankness. But my eyes don't leave her tiny body crumpled and tossed in between the empty rows like garbage.

'We have to go, now.' Paltino tugs me out of Axalte's hold and shakes me. 'Go to Una, Axalte. I got her.' Paltino's right. Axalte has exposed himself and he has to hide but he isn't ready. I don't think he thought this through. Not that I blame him. I would have done the same thing.

'Go, Axalte.' I push against him but like a rooted tree but he doesn't budge. He slips his hand to the back of my neck and gently pulls me into him. He buries his nose into my hair between my ear and my neck and inhales me. When he lets me go, both of us somehow know that he's really letting me go.

The door flies open and ten officers file in, guns first. We can't take all of them. They don't know about us, Paltino. They just know about Axalte and they can't see feral wild child's body between these rows. Paltino nods.

I grab Axalte's arm and puff my chest. 'About time you arrived. Look at this. Look how many officers we lost.' I flail my arms at the dead and blank officers who bump into each other and trip over dead bodies periodically. The officers bow their heads to me in respect.

'Forgive me, but shouldn't we terminate this man if he is such a danger?' one of the officers tests me. He must be the leader of the group.

'He is not the danger. It's the girl. She's a Mark. And you're wasting time because she escaped through those doors heading west.' Paltino points to a set of doors on the other side of the auditorium. The officers shift in their positions, scratching heads, arching backs, adjusting their grips on their guns, unsure of what they should do. A blank officer walks into a wall and bounces off on to the floor. They are all fuddling robots and zombies, washed or not.

'Did you both see her? The Mark?' the leader respectfully questions.

'No, I saw her. The Expert here was busy apprehending this rogue officer.' Paltino's voice is louder that it normally is; he's protecting me again. Lying that only he saw the Mark so that if anything happens it will be on him, not me. But the leader is not buying it. Axalte pretends to be stuck in my grip and fakes a struggle to break free.

'No, leave her alone. Don't go after her. She's just a kid.' Axalte's lip twitches and his eyebrows droop. I don't think it was hard for him to pretend to care for feral wild child . . . as if his pleading for her life would change the fact that she's already dead.

'Shut up!' I bash my elbow into Axalte's mouth. I pull the hit but I split his lip and blood pours out and down his chin. It looks a lot worse than it is. They are buying it now. I turn back to the officers. 'Did you not hear the orders? The Mark has run that way. Follow her. Don't make me remind you of your rank, officer.' Teen Me's voice does not shake. Transmit, receive, process. The leader shudders a bow and head-gestures for eight of the ten officers to follow the Mark.

There's three left. We can definitely take these three; we just need to synchronize our attack. But before I can get Paltino's attention, the leader has already walked over to him and is shaking his hand. The leader is herding Paltino backwards towards us, towards feral wild child's body. Paltino is unarmed and the two other officers have circled the auditorium and are behind us.

The leader spouts pleasantries and Paltino reciprocates but they are getting too close to her body. If the leader sees her body he will know Paltino lied and his identity will be as lost as Axalte's.

'Officer Paltino, let's take this Riser scum in,' I interrupt.

'Excellent, Expert.' Paltino quickly agrees and spins on his heels to rush over to us when the leader wraps his hands around Paltino's neck and squeezes. The leader's eyes are fixed on feral wild child's mangled body.

'Expert, it seems that this officer was covering for the Riser scum. That girl didn't escape. Her dead body is right there.' The leader squeezes harder and Paltino's face blues. 'We are authorized to terminate them both, Expert.'

That's why Paltino said only he saw the Mark. They don't expect anything of me. Axalte shakes his head at me. He knows what I'm going to do.

'Don't expose yourself, Suni,' Axalte whispers.

'What? Do you think I am just going to sit here and watch him die? Not me. Not ever,' Teen Me thunders as wind twists and turns around her, lashing her hair as the leader and the two other officers burst into flames, shriek and fumble around the room, setting fire to everything they touch until their shrills and the fire burn out.

Unpredictable, uncontrollable fire. I'm a Mark.

# Chapter 39

I'm a Mark. Axalte holds Paltino by the neck and squeezes.
This is what he was anticipating. He knew. He knew I
was a Mark. He knew I wouldn't just sit here and watch
him die. He knew strangling Paltino would trigger that
memory. He knew because he's Axalte. The real Axalte.
The reclaim worked. It worked just like Teen Me knew it
would. But he must not have had a memory until . . . the
kiss. The bloody kiss was the trigger. I brought you back.
I found a way.

My love does mean faith.

I am not done yet. There's a lot more left in me. The
corner of my mouth pinches into a side smile. It's Teen
Me. He sees her. I see her. I am Teen Me, after all. Axalte
drops Paltino. Fellie's voice replays in my head over and
over again—'*Own my pain. Own your pain. It will set you
ablaze and your wildfire will spread throughout Pangea.*'

Wind churns around me like a gentle tornado. This
skin, this new skin is warm and tingly and the fire that burns

through my veins is so alive it possesses me. I don't fight it. I let it take over and fill in all the achy, broken parts of me. Sexy, spunky, cheeky, uncontrollable, unpredictable me. I like it. No, I love it.

All I have to do is look at a Hunter or an officer and they light up like tumbleweed in the sun, tumbling and screeching rootless balls of fire. One, two. Axalte injects Paltino with something that wakes him. Three, four. The burning Hunters roll into gurneys, slam into walls and spread the fire faster than I could. Well, not *faster* than I could. Uncontrollable, unpredictable fire. Where's Joyli?

*Paltino: She went to get her doses.*

I can hear Paltino? Yes, I can hear Paltino. I'm a Mark and all Marks can connect . . . that's how he's been hearing me all this time. I was just not ready to see that I could hear him too. Hey, Paltino I'm so glad you're not dead.

I open my hands wide and feel the flames pull out of my palms like flickering tickles until they swirl into large throbbing orbs of fire. I sling them, make more and repeat until the entire lab is swallowed by my ravenous whirling flames.

*Paltino: I'm so glad that you remembered who you are. Took you long enough.*

Axalte scoops me up in his woody embrace and buries his nose in my hair to inhale me. He bats his eyelashes. The real Axalte with the real Suni. And just like that, all is right with the world.

'We need to get out of here before his wife gets back all dosed up.' Paltino pats Axalte on the back. 'Good to see you being you.' Axalte flashes his toothy grin that we haven't seen in forever.

'I've got maybe one jump left. Don't think there's enough juice to get very far. But let's do this. Come here, princess, I missed you too. Well, I would have if I'd remembered you existed.' Axalte pulls Princess Paltino on to one side and me on to the other.

'I thought you said you could only carry one person in a teleport?' I ask.

'I lied.' Axalte throws a shrug-grin combo. There's a little new Axalte in the real Axalte now.

The ceiling collapses, showering the lab with concrete and dust, smothering out most of my fire. Joyli jumps through the hazy dust smoke and prowls back and forth in her pre-attack predatory dance, her eyes glowing blue, her veins pulsing across her neck, cheek, forehead and her body twitching as if every cell of every muscle wants nothing other than to rip me to pieces.

It starts with a nervous jittery feeling in my fingertips and then it shoots up my body with deep, sharp electric claws piercing through me, into my bones, sending needly shivers up into my skull. Psycho-electrocution. The electricity clamps its jaws into my spine and shakes, hammering my teeth together, snapping my head back and forth, tangling and untangling my limbs like floppy string. I can't see. I can't hear. I can't feel.

Just when I find the desire to live again, just when I find something to live for I find myself dying. And at the hands of the monster I created with the power of the Mark I unleashed. But I'm not broken, achy Pangean Me. I'm not going to cry and wallow in fate's bad timing. I'm not going to count my scars and I sure as hell am not going to feel sorry for myself. I own my pain. I own my fate. I own my death. I'm pissed as all hell because I'm not ready to go. I spit in death's face. I spit in the world's face. I spit in The Creator's face.

Feral wild child, this world was not made for you and I.

# Chapter 40

*Paltino: It's time to run, Suni.*

*I take one last long look at feral wild child's tossed body before Axalte tears me away. We hurdle over burning corpses and scramble towards Paltino at the door. How many people did Teen Me kill in that auditorium?*

*We troop out of the door and wind between the narrow streets, ploughing through Pangeans muddling and fumbling in their assigned routines. Officers can't be far behind. We have just a few more streets until we are at the wall and then the desert and then the tunnels. They can't keep up once we reach the tunnels. Run harder.*

*I glance over my shoulder. Twenty, maybe thirty officers round the corner. They're close. The wall is in sight but we can't make it. If we stop at the wall to burn out an opening, they will catch up to us.*

*Paltino: Burn them, burn them all, Suni.*

*Kill them? Thirty more? What about all the Pangeans in the street? Unpredictable, uncontrollable fire would kill them too.*

*How many more people need to die for us to live? Even Teen Me can't stomach it. I think I have killed enough for one day. I stretch my palm open.*

*Paltino: Don't, Suni!*

*Axalte doesn't need to hear my thoughts to know them. He shakes his head at me, hoping that for this one time I will listen to him. They don't want me to reveal myself as a Mark. I'd have to be in hiding. What they don't understand is that I can't stay in Pangea without Axalte. If he's in hiding then I'm in hiding. Where he is, is where I will always be. Always.*

*I spin flames in my palms in a circular dance, feeding them and growing them until they form bubbling balls of fiery lava and catapult them into the wall. A symphony of Pangean shrieks, yelps and squeals crescendo amidst the clicks of officers' guns being readied while babies are scooped up and shuffled away from the Mark monster. Transmit, receive, process. Thirty guns, thirty clicks. The wall's burning plastic oozes a gluey opening just big enough for us to dive through. I cast a blast of fire between us and the officers that erupts up and with nothing to burn fizzles down into a black cloud of smoke— it buys us just enough time to get through the wall—just dive through it, Paltino!*

*He does, then Axalte, then me. Guns fire! I spring up and halfway through the hole a bullet drives in and out of my leg and I slump into the sand. Sand slaps me in the face. I can't see. I can't breathe. I can't move. Sandstorm.*

*I feel Axalte's arm take mine and pull me up. A grinding pain sears through my leg. It's the sand burrowing into my wound like millions of hungry night ants. I drag my sinking legs through the sand but even with Axalte hauling me forward I'm slow, much slower than I would be. The officers must be through the hole now. I have to see.*

*I open my eyes just a slit and try to keep blinking out the sharp stinging sand. Axalte buries his face in his arm and tries to drudge forward with me in tow. I can barely make out a figure some twenty feet ahead. It's Paltino. I'm slowing Axalte down by twenty feet.*

*I turn around. The sand slices into my exposed cheek and neck but I have to see. The officers. They are just a few steps behind me. They will get us.*

*Paltino: Suni, you have to burn them. You have no choice.*

*I try to set them ablaze. But I can't. The strong winds blow out my flames like a simple candle and the sand smothers my spark. You don't go in a sandstorm. You never go in a sandstorm. I cannot go on and I cannot let them take Axalte.*

*Paltino: They know you're a Mark. They won't wash you, Suni. They will kill you.*

*Better me than Axalte. Take care of him, Paltino. I jerk my arm away from Axalte and turn towards the officers. They just want me. They won't keep risking this sandstorm for mere Risers. But I'm a Mark. A powerful Mark. They are here for me and after they have me Axalte and Paltino can escape.*

*I have to walk into an officer before he sees me. He clamps me by my shoulder and pushes me to the ground, knee in my* back. *Two officers huddle around me and their boots shelter me from the wind just enough for me to open my eyes but not enough for my fire. They know this is the only way to kill me, out here in the sandstorm where I have no power. Feral wild child, this world was not made for you and I.*

*But I don't die here. I know I don't die here because I'm still alive. They wash me here instead of killing me? Why would they do that? Why would they keep such a powerful Mark alive? It was The Creator, wasn't it? He's been watching me, toying with me. Did they herd me out here into the sandstorm knowing I would be powerless here? Have I been living under the same illusion of control this whole time? How long have I been playing his game?*

*Paltino: Suni?*

*The other officers must be close behind. What is taking them so long? Why don't they just do it and be done? The longer they take, the more time Axalte and Paltino have to escape. Take your time, robots. Take your time.*

*The sand-scarred winds howl and through my fissured eyes I can barely make out one of the officers, the one with his knee in my back, slide out his gun—not his stunray—not his Washer— his gun. I don't die here. I know I don't die here.*

*In one fluid dance-like move he sticks the gun into the other officer's neck, pulls the trigger and the sand-clawed squalls carry away the sprayed blood and brains. Who is the shooter? A Riser? He slides his knee out of my back and into the sand beside me as he bends close to me. I still can't see everything but I can see that* his face is creviced like the walls of a cave. He's old. The oldest man I have ever seen. Who are you?

Shooter: A messenger.

Me: Who sent you?

Shooter: I am to tell you that your brother is alive. He's in the outer limits, outside Pangea. You are to go to him. He has waited for you for a long time. That is my message. That is my purpose.

Me: Hayk is alive? He's alive?

I try to turn and rise out of the sand but the shooter's heavy hand pushes me back in the sand.

Me: What are you doing? I'm to go to him! You said I am to go!

Shooter: No. You must remain here.

Me: What? What is point of telling me to go Hayk and then leave me here to die?

Shooter: You will not die here. You will be washed.

Me: And me knowing that Hayk is alive, will be washed away? Why would you tell me just for it to be washed? You just want to torment me? Is that your purpose?

Shooter: No. The message is not for you. Not the 'you' that you know now. It is for the 'you' that you will become.

Me. The message is for me. Not Teen Me. Me.

The herd of officers heaves through the sand just an arm's length away. I squirm, writhe, wriggle, punch, kick. I am trapped. Trapped under the shooter's weight, trapped by the storm, trapped by the officers, and choking. Choking on the sand *clawing inside my throat, choking on my cracked screams and choking on the loss of my brother, again.*

The shooter's hand snaps up to his vest and pulls on a lever that releases a parachute behind him. A white cloud silently mushrooms on its strings before it and the shooter vanishes into the rabid storm just as the knees and elbows of the herd of officers dig into my back, the back of my skull and my limbs.

Other officers push Axalte down into the sand next to me. Our barely opened sand-beaten eyes meet. He frees one arm and traces a line from my eyebrow to my chin. Where he is, is where I will be, always.

An officer bashes the back of his gun into Axalte's free elbow and even in the deafening moans of the sandstorm I can hear the crack. Axalte's face grips in pain. This is where I lose him. This is where I lose myself.

*Find him, Paltino. Promise me you will find both of them.* The officer pries the narrow slit of my eyelids open with a Washer.

Teen Me shakes her head and slams her forehead into the Washer. She'd rather die than get washed. They can take her life, but she won't let them take her mind. She tries to light the Washer on fire but her sparks are carried away by the stormy winds. She won't let them turn her into an empty bobblehead. She opens her mouth and chokes on sand as she clamps her jaw on to the officer's wrist. She won't let them make her a programmed robot. The officer squeals and drops the Washer. She won't let them take her fire. Another officer shoves the heel of his boot into her cheek and kicks her face back to the ground.

*She won't let them take her brother. She screams through her sand-filled mouth as the officer jams the Washer into her eye and squeezes. She won't let them make her . . . me.*

*The sky, the sun, the storm, the winds, the world, everything down to the very last thing Teen Me sees—Axalte's thickly-lashed almond eyes—is swallowed by total and complete blackness.*

*I did die here.*

# Chapter 41

I do die here.

It's cold and I'm so tired but I can't sleep. I can't. The winking eye, the moon painted on my ceiling. The breaking smile. Were those always yours, Hayk? Was that always you who came back to me in the sleepy, lonely hours? And those cries—those chest-squeezing cries. They smother me and I can't breathe. I want to sleep. I just want to sleep. But I can't. Not yet. Not now that I know you're alive, Hayk. That message was for me. You have been waiting for me. I am not going to sleep. Not now. I am coming, Hayk. I am coming.

And that's when I feel Axalte's arm at the dip of my waist slide across to my chest. Catch my breath, Axalte. Catch my breath.

My eyes open to the blinding carnivorous sun and Axalte's wide hands pumping my chest. I suck in as much air as my lungs will hold and blow out as much my lungs will blow. I do this a few times as if I need to remind myself how to do it. As soon as I get the hang of it my body wrings into a retch as I heave whatever I have left in my stomach—nothing. That's it. I have definitely thrown up way too much in the last three days.

We are in the desert, just a couple of hundred feet from the headquarters. Axalte and Paltino are tensed up, faces red, eyes puffy, eyebrows knitted. We must have teleported out at some point and then they tried to revive me, I guess. Judging by their faces, it's been a while. How long was I dead?

They take turns bear-hugging me and all I can focus on is the burning floor of the headquarters that fills the sky with plumes of grey smoke. There's someone in there, standing there in the fire, staring at us. It's Joyli. Through the smoke, through the flames I can see her electric blue eyes jolting with hunger, unshaken by the fact that the rest of her is burning alive. She wants me dead more that she wants to live and she has every right to feel that way. I took her life with a promise of a better life and then I took that life from her too.

I don't know if it's because it's the right thing to do or if it's because I can't bear the sight of Joyli anymore but I set the entire headquarters ablaze. I'm not sure I even think about it as much as I should. I guess I am getting more and more at ease with my comfort with killing. Unpredictable, uncontrollable fire. The flames fight the sun to paint the sky in reds, yellows and oranges. My flames fight the sun.

'Don't kill her, Suni.' Axalte sinks his heavy hand into my shoulder.

'She won't stop coming after us.' He knows I'm right but it's nice to have him back. The him I remember. The him I love.

'I'll find a way to reclaim her, Suni.' Teen Me wouldn't have taken the chance. She would have burned down the entire city to be on the safe side. But Teen Me died that day in the sandstorm. The day I was born. And with a flick of the wrist my flames withdraw as Axalte shades me in his woody embrace.

I could wilt into Axalte's hold and recount the ways he remained with me even during my wash. How my gut never ceased aching, how I counted trees and how I felt his love in warm mint tea. Or twine my fingers with Paltino's and soothe him with how much I actually do need him and would throw myself for him again and again. But I don't.

I could get wound up in all the open questions: Why The Creator did all this, why he hides or why he asked about my mother. Who was the shooter, how did he know I would recall that memory when I did or even that I would be reclaimed and how could he have been so old? Am I really married to Toke? What are the outer limits? How are we going to get there to find Hayk and what are we going to have to fight to get to him? But I don't.

Not yet. Right now, I'm just going to drink in this moment and fill my head with dreams of sour pie, crusty breads with soft, warm centres, a tall glass of really cold water and a long well-deserved night's sleep.

# Acknowledgements

I'd like to thank everyone at Penguin Random House India for all their hard work in making this book a success and a special thanks to all my friends and family that read, reread and re-reread this book, giving me notes along the way.

My editor, Ameya Nagarajan, thank you for duking this out with me every step of the way and letting me hound you via whatsapp.

It all began with my parents, my inspiration. Thank you for always believing in a little girl's daydreams. Abba, you are the rock that all the men in my writing and in my life are measured against. Poor guys, never had a chance. Moma, you're an amazing human being with a heart as big as an ocean. I can only wish to be a fraction of the mother you are. I love you.

Daniyal, my son, my moon and my stars, I turned to you when I was stuck in a storyline, needed to spice stuff up or just wanted to pull my hair out. You are very much a part of this book. Now you may want to read it, ahem.

Dyana, your fire inspired Suni's. You have so many gifts that you haven't been able to see yet. Always remember who you are and how much I love you. *Duck face, peace sign*.

Hamza, I'm sorry that I ignored you while I wrote this but I did buy you a ton of Lego sets so I'm pretty sure you forgave me. I love you to the moon.

My husband. Hassan, I don't know how to write love without writing you. You have read (eventually) every page of every draft of every version of everything I have written even though I would yell at you for not giving me enough feedback. You restored my faith in humanity. Thank you for loving me.

And finally, I have to thank the One who cannot be named. I don't remember you as much as I should yet you are always there for me. Thank you for all you have given me. Without you, I am nothing.